RUGBY REBEL

GERARD SIGGINS

THE O'BRIEN PRESS
DUBLIN

First published 2015 by
The O'Brien Press Ltd,
12 Terenure Road East, Rathgar,
Dublin 6, D06 HD27, Ireland.
Tel: +353 1 4923333; Fax: +353 1 4922777
E-mail: books@obrien.ie.
Website: www.obrien.ie
Reprinted 2016.

ISBN: 978-1-84717-677-6

8 7 6 5 4 3 2
18 17 16

Printed and bound by CPI Group (UK) Ltd, Croydon, CR0 4YY
The paper in this book is produced using pulp from managed forests

The O'Brien Press receives financial assistance from

DEDICATION

My family have always given my books great support, and I would like to dedicate *Rugby Rebel* to them. Thank you Auntie Eileen, Auntie Carmel and Auntie Dor, and Uncle Jim and Uncle David.

ACKNOWLEDGEMENTS

The three ghosts in this series, Brian Hanrahan, Dave Gallaher and Kevin Barry, all once lived and I have treated the facts of them and their lives with respect, while obviously taking some liberties with their speech. The story of the fourth ghost, Eugene McCann, is not based on any character or episode from history.

I would also like to acknowledge Donal O'Donovan's book *Kevin Barry And His Time* (Glendale, 1989), which helped me to get a fuller picture of the man.

I would like to thank all at The O'Brien Press for their help, especially my wonderful editor Helen Carr, brilliant designer Emma Byrne, and Ruth Heneghan and Bronagh McDermott in the publicity department.

Thanks also to the many schools, libraries and bookshops that have invited me to talk about Brian, Eoin and the stories behind the stories. The people that work in these places play such an important role in passing on the gift of reading.

As do parents, and especially mine. Thanks Da, thanks Mam.

Chapter 1

· · · · · · · · ·

'**D**UCK!' came the call from somewhere to Eoin's left. He instinctively lowered his head just as a bullet whizzed over his helmet.

'That was close,' he muttered as he adjusted his head-gear. He gripped his rifle tightly and turned to where the call had come from. A burly man with a black moustache grinned back at him.

'You still have a few days' rugby left in you yet, son,' he chuckled.

'Rugby?' said Eoin, suddenly remembering. 'Oh no, I'm late!' he called, as he swung his legs out of bed.

Putting on his socks, Eoin paused, recalling the last moments of his dream.

'Saved me again, Dave, didn't you?' he grinned, looking over at the precious piece of black cloth which carried an embroidered silver fern, and which now lay behind a pane of glass on his bedroom wall.

Eoin had been having plenty of dreams that summer after a memorable and moving school visit to the World War One battlefields; he'd won the trip for his whole class as a prize in the Young Historian Competition.

His winning project had been inspired by a famous New Zealand rugby player whose ghost had appeared to Eoin and given him some very useful help.

Eoin hadn't expected to meet Dave Gallaher again, but Eoin's dreams had recently resembled vivid chapters from Dave's war stories.

Being able to see and talk to the dead was something that still didn't make huge sense to Eoin. He hadn't really believed in ghosts, but now he was friends with two – Brian and Dave – and saw nothing strange in that. Brian Hanrahan had died in a scrum in Lansdowne Road many years before; he was only twenty-two when he died and was a real mentor to Eoin now – especially when it came to rugby.

Eoin wasn't sure quite how he had this special gift, but his friend Alan had been able to see Brian too at a moment of great danger last term and he wondered had that anything to do with it.

Eoin ran downstairs into the kitchen where his mother was shovelling a large mound of bacon and sausage onto a plate.

'Ah, just in time, Eoin,' she smiled, 'I was just about to call you again.'

'Sorry, Mum,' he replied,. 'I have to meet Dylan down the field for a bit of rugby. But keep that for me, please,' as he swiped one sausage from the plate and sped out the door.

Eoin jogged the short distance to the Ormondstown Gaels ground where his pal Dylan was waiting impatiently.

'Do you know how many times I've kicked this wall?' he asked.

'Eighty-three?' grinned Eoin.

'Not funny. Look at the state of my boots! Lucky I'm getting a new pair for my birthday next week,' said Dylan.

'Nobody asked you to kick the wall,' Eoin replied. 'Why didn't you do something useful like kick the heads off the nettles?'

'Ah, will you two ever stop that,' laughed Barney, the Gaels' groundsman. 'And do you call those things "boots"?' he added. 'Ask your grandfather to show you a pair of his boots, Eoin. They were the real thing.'

Eoin smiled and nodded at old Barney. 'I don't think Grandad has any of his old boots still, but I've seen them in photos. Big, heavy things like climbing boots, weren't they?'

'They were indeed. We used them for all sports, and

once your feet had stopped growing they were yours for life,' the old man said. 'You could plant a free or a rugby penalty from anywhere with a boot like that.'

The boys laughed along with Barney, who had been the heart and soul of the Gaels as long as they remembered, and long before that. All summer long Eoin and Dylan had played Gaelic football and hurling, but every morning for the last month they had started a bit of rugby practice on their own. One or two members of the Gaels had muttered to Barney that rugby shouldn't be allowed on the GAA pitch, but he told them to mind their own business and, sure, wasn't it helping the lads in their GAA skills anyway?

Eoin hoofed the ball high into the air and Dylan set off in pursuit like a demented puppy. He ran one way, and stepped sideways a couple of times trying to get under the ball as the strong breeze tugged at it on its descent. At the last second it seemed to drift away further, but Dylan dived forward and held the ball just before it hit the ground.

'Yes!' he roared. 'And Ormondstown have won the Ashes!'

Eoin laughed. 'You might make a decent cricketer yet, but if this was a rugby match you'd be already buried under five or six big forwards.'

The pair went through a few moves before Eoin spent the last fifteen minutes of their session taking kicks at goal, with Dylan happy to run around collecting the ball.

'All set for next week?' Eoin asked his pal.

'Yeah, the uniform still fits me, which is a bit depressing,' Dylan replied.

'Well you'll be fine then unless GI Joe wants it back,' Eoin quipped, before skipping out of reach as Dylan took a swipe.

'Come back here, you big lug,' Dylan roared, as the pair charged out of the grounds, laughing all the way.

Chapter 2

· · · · · · · · ·

'DYLAN really seems to have settled down,' Eoin's mum announced after tea.

'Yeah, I suppose so,' said Eoin. 'Once that thing with his dad was sorted out he's been in great form. He's really put it behind him and it's been good crack to have him around for the summer.'

Eoin and Dylan had been involved in a dramatic incident at Lansdowne Road at the previous season's schools' cup final, but they had escaped with no harm done.

'There's a big weight off his shoulders, I'm sure,' his mother chipped in.

'Yeah, I suppose,' Eoin replied, before turning to his father. 'Did you ever notice how mam never asks questions?' he grinned. 'She just puts a statement out there and expects you to comment, like she's on one of those TV politics shows or something …'

His father chuckled. 'Well, now that you mention it …' he started, cautiously.

He was cut off by a flying tea towel as Mrs Madden

stood up in mock fury.

'How dare you, young man, and me after cooking you a lovely meal too!'

'Sorry, Mam, I was only having a laugh. But if they had you on the telly I'd definitely watch it!' Eoin replied, as he fled from a second tea towel spearing in his direction.

He trotted upstairs to his bedroom, which was in the middle of a major overhaul. Most of his clothes were on the bed, and he had a large plastic sack into which he had been tossing the old toys and books he had decided he wouldn't miss. All the old bedtime story books had been replaced by new books on the things he was interested in, such as rugby, ghosts and history.

He picked up a coaching book his grandfather had given him for his birthday and studied one of the diagrams. It was all very well seeing a slick move like that printed on a page, but what were the chances of the Castlerock team executing it? As the old coach Mr Finn used to say, 'Keep it simple'.

He lay down and stared at the ceiling. It was funny how the first two years at Castlerock had gone for him. He had been terrified at first, and having to take up rugby only added to his nightmares in those early weeks at the boarding school. But, in a funny way, it was playing the game that helped him to settle in and make friends. Now it was his main passion and everyone said he had turned into a decent player too.

But this was going to be a big year at Castlerock. Devin, the captain of the Junior Cup team, had come up to him in the schoolyard just before the summer break and told him he wanted him in his squad. Eoin was excited by the idea of playing in a huge competition like that – and he knew how seriously they took the 'Js' at the school.

It was also the start of the state exams cycle and his mum had been nagging him all summer about how important it was to get good results in the exam, and how he would have to work steadily over the two years. The arrival of his school report kept her quiet for a day or two, but she soon started picking holes in the results and pointing out where he would have to turn those B minuses into B pluses.

Eoin laughed, still amazed at how positive the school report had been, but he reckoned it was his win in the national Young Historian Competition that had given the teachers such a good impression of him. It was even funnier to remember how he had been bored by history in primary school – it was learning more about the past through his ghostly pals that had sparked his new interest.

I wonder will they give us another project this year? he thought. *I wouldn't mind having something like that to keep me busy.'*

He divided the last of his old belongings between a cardboard box, to be stored in the attic, and the plastic sack, to be taken to the charity shop. There were some hard decisions, and he realised he hadn't a clue what would mean most to him about his childhood far in the future. He shrugged his shoulders and decided not to think about it too deeply, consigning mementoes of his first thirteen years on earth into the 'keep' or 'lose' piles on a whim.

Chapter 3

· · · · · · · · ·

THE last few days of freedom went quickly, as they always do. Eoin stuffed his books into his schoolbag and crammed the sports gear in a large Munster Rugby holdall, while his mother neatly folded his carefully ironed uniform and casual clothes into a large suitcase.

'Ah, don't iron the socks, Mam, the lads give me an awful time about that,' he said.

She smiled. 'Don't be worrying about that. It's nice to look nice, although I don't imagine your pals would notice. Have you everything packed?'

'Think so,' replied Eoin. 'I'm just going to run up to say goodbye to Grandad.'

'I do believe he's just saved you a journey,' she replied, as she pointed out the window to where his grandfather, the great Dixie Madden, was standing, waving up at them.

Eoin lugged the two bags over his shoulder and struggled downstairs and out to the car.

'Hello, young man,' said Dixie. 'All set for Castlerock?'

'I suppose so.' said Eoin, 'Are you coming up for the spin?'

'I'd love to, but there's not enough room with you and your pal and all those bags.'

'Oh, I'd forgotten all about Dylan. Where is he?' asked Eoin, looking out the gate.

'I've given his mam a ring,' said Eoin's father. 'We'll call by his house and pick him up.'

'Well, Eoin, I hope this school year won't be quite as dramatic as the last one.' said Dixie, 'Although I do hope we get another trip up to the Viva Stadium.'

'Ah, Grandad, you never get that right – it's the A-viva,' laughed Eoin.

'Oh well, it will always be Lansdowne Road to me,' chuckled his grandad.

'Well, I wouldn't get your hopes up, Grandad. I'd be really lucky to even make the Junior Cup panel – it's unheard of in second year. I'll have another go at it after this year though so keep taking your cod liver oil tablets!'

Dixie laughed and slipped a banknote into Eoin's pocket.

Eoin smiled and gave the old man a hug. 'Thanks, Grandad, I've had my eye on the new Ireland jersey for ages. I'll be able to get it now.'

'Oh, sure can't you wait till you're selected – they'll give you any number of jerseys then for free!'

Eoin laughed aloud. 'Thanks, Grandad, no pressure!'

With all the bags loaded in the boot, Eoin turned to give his mother one last hug and hopped into the front seat beside his dad.

'See you all at Hallowe'en!' he called as the car pulled out of the drive and turned towards Ormondstown town centre.

'It's great that Dylan's going back to Castlerock,' said his dad. 'He should be a lot more content this year too.'

'I hope so.' replied Eoin, 'He's been in good form all summer and seems mad keen to get back. I hope we can keep the rugby going too.'

'Yes. I expect it will be tricky this year with you pushing for the JCT squad. Will any of the rest of the lads be in contention?' asked Dad.

'It's hard to know. The squad's weak enough in the backs, so Richie Duffy might get called up too, maybe Mikey O'Reilly. Dylan's still very small though …' Eoin ventured.

'And here is the pocket rocket himself,' said Mr Madden, as he eased the car up against the kerb. Dylan was standing outside the house where he lived with his mam and sister Caoimhe.

'Howya, Mr Madden,' called Dylan, as he started lugging his bags across the footpath to the car.

Eoin's dad stepped out to help Dylan, while Eoin stuck his head in through the doorway.

'We're off, Mrs Coonan,' he called, as Dylan's mother and sister came into the hallway. Caoimhe was carrying a tray.

'I cooked some sausage rolls for you for the journey,' she said.

'Oh, that's fantastic!' said Eoin. 'You're a total legend, Caoi!'

Dylan's sister blushed. 'There's two each, don't let Dylan have any more, he's been raiding the oven all morning.'

Eoin grabbed the sausage rolls, gave the pair a wave and hopped back in the car as Dylan gave his mam and sister a hug.

'Be good, work hard and keep in touch,' were his mother's last orders as he rolled up the window and the car zoomed off in the direction of Dublin.

Chapter 4

. . . .

THE first night back after the summer holidays was always an exciting one for Eoin and his friends. Which dormitory they had been allocated was the most important bit of information to be gleaned and Eoin was delighted that he had once again been pitched in with Rory, Alan and Dylan in smaller, four-bed sleeping quarters.

'Hey, Madden, there's a shocking smell of farmyard off you,' came a voice from under the bed he had claimed.

'Alan, don't tell me you've lost your mouse again?' asked Eoin.

Alan stood up. 'No, and thanks for mentioning it. He ran away during the summer. I think the cat got him. No, I was under the bed checking out a funny-looking trapdoor – see?'

Eoin peered under the bed, where sure enough there was a square hole cut in the planks. Alan was trying to lift it, but it seemed to have been painted shut by many coats of varnish.

'Oh well, I thought there might be a secret passageway downstairs we could have used to raid the kitchen during the night,' he sighed.

'Still thinking of your belly, Al?' laughed Dylan. 'Did you get to the gym much over the summer?'

Alan glowered, but Eoin stepped in. 'Leave it out, Dyl, you were fairly guzzling the sausage rolls yourself earlier.'

Dylan laughed again. 'Only messing, lads, sure it's great we're all back together here. Wonder who Kevin and Fiachra have been put in with?'

'They're next door with Hugh Bowers and Pearse Hickey,' Alan replied. 'That sounds like a fun room to be in.'

'As long as they keep the noise down,' said Eoin. 'I've spent most of the summer sleeping. I'm getting very fond of my naps. Mr Carey said they're vital for top-class sportsmen.'

Eoin claimed a bed beside the door and lay down. His peace lasted just a moment, however, as a t-shirt came flying across the room and landed right on his face.

'Yuk, that's stinking!' he cried.

'Sorry, Eoin! I borrowed that off you last term,' said Rory. 'It's been at the bottom of the bag ever since. I kept meaning to ask Mam to wash it but ….'

Eoin felt like exploding, but he had found that it was

usually better to walk away any time he felt like that. This was one of those occasions.

'OK, no worries, Rory, but it's obvious I'm not going to get much sleep here,' snapped Eoin as he stormed out the door.

Eoin set off down the stairs at a jog, but he stopped short when he saw Mr Carey, the rugby coach, coming up towards him.

'Be careful there, Madden,' the teacher said. 'You could have sent me flying.'

'Sorry, sir,' he replied.

'I was on my way up to see you. How do you feel about training with the JCT squad this year?'

'Eh … well, OK, I suppose,' stammered Eoin.

'Devin Synnott – he's the J's captain – told me he wants you on the team. I'm not sure about that. You're very young and still a bit raw, but I'm prepared to give you a go until Christmas. They can probably spare you on the Under 14s but you might have to play a few extra games. As you've no major exams this year, that shouldn't be a problem. Are you OK with that?'

Although Eoin had known Devin wanted him to train with the Js, he was still a bit taken aback by Mr Carey's approach. He hadn't expected to be called up to train with them so soon and wasn't at all sure about this development.

'Of course, yes, OK,' said Eoin. 'When do they train?'

'We start tomorrow for two hours after school, then it's an hour every day and two on Saturday mornings unless you've a match. Sunday is your own. We'll probably start the pre-school sessions after Christmas.'

Eoin's mouth opened, but he didn't know what to say. He just nodded and said thanks before continuing down the stairs and out the front door.

He jogged away to his favourite place in Castlerock, the secluded corner of the woods where a tiny stream bubbled its way down to the sea. There was a large rock he liked to sit on and think; it provided a rare oasis of peace in the bustling boarding school.

The Rock was empty, as it always was. Eoin had never seen anyone down this part of the school, except of course his ghostly friends Brian and Dave, who seemed to be drawn to the place. Eoin wondered about that – was there something about the site that the ghosts liked? It certainly had a very different atmosphere to the rest of the school.

It was a warm evening and Eoin was tired after the exertions and excitement of the day. He sat down on his favourite rock and closed his eyes. It was good to get such time alone. He thought back to the last time he had been there, and ...

'*Crack!*'

He was brought back to reality by a loud noise that sounded almost like a gunshot.

'*Crack!*'

There it was again, even nearer this time. He was sure it was a gunshot this time.

Eoin ran out of the tiny wooded area, terrified. He looked around, but couldn't work out what had caused the noise. It seemed to come from the side of the school. He turned towards the front of the old, grey school building and ran towards it as fast as his legs would let him.

Once he got to the doorway he paused and looked back, but there was no sign of the gunman. Eoin gulped down breaths, trying to calm himself down after the scary experience. *Did I imagine that?* he thought. *Would Mr McCaffrey think I'm telling lies?*

Eoin decided to keep it to himself, and trudged nervously upstairs.

Chapter 5

· · · · · · · · ·

IF the first night in the dorm was exciting, the same couldn't really be said for the first day of classes. It might have been a little bit interesting to find out who each of their new teachers would be, but it wasn't long before the novelty was lost on the boys, especially when so many of the teachers were keen on getting down to work immediately.

'Remember, this is second year, the start of your Junior Cert cycle,' said Mr McAllister, the Irish teacher. 'I'll have to check out how you've all been doing over the last year. We'll have a little test on Friday.'

The class groaned. They might be back at school, but for many their minds were still at home or away on holiday. It would be hard to focus on an exam in week one – but maybe that was Mr McAllister's idea.

The first day dragged like a wet Sunday afternoon in February. But Eoin was happy that it did, because he was more than a little nervous about the Js' training session – and about telling the rest of his team-mates that he wouldn't be seeing much of them this year.

After the last class was over, Eoin gathered his rugby gear and sauntered out the classroom door.

'Wait up, Eoin, where you off to?' asked Rory.

'I've got rugby,' he replied.

Rory looked puzzled. 'But they said we wouldn't be starting up till next week?'

'Mr Carey wants me to train with the Js,' he muttered.

The rest of his pals stopped and stared.

'You can't be! You're only in second year – second years never train with the Js,' said Alan.

'No, it's not that rare,' lied Eoin. 'And anyway, nothing might come of it. They've a half-decent side this year, I think.'

'But what about the 14s?' asked Dylan, 'We'll be useless without you!'

'Ah come off it, Richie Duffy can slot in for me, and I can probably play a lot of the games anyway. I better run, you know what Carey can be like if you're late.'

Eoin trotted over to the changing room, and followed the rest of the players inside. He recognised many of them, but no one said anything to him. He looked around desperately for Devin Synnott, the captain, who didn't seem to be about.

They're not a very friendly bunch, are they? he thought to himself.

He put on his kit and wandered outside, where Devin was talking to Mr Carey. Devin was the star of the Js panel, and a year ahead of Eoin.

'Ah, Eoin, thanks for coming. I was just working out with Mr Carey what we'd do with you. We've a big squad this year, but we don't have much cover at out-half if Ronan goes down. We're going to play a trial today so we'll slot you in at inside centre for the first half and switch you with Paudie for the second. Is that OK?'

Eoin nodded and suddenly felt extra nervous. He was big enough for his age, but these guys just looked much bigger than his old team-mates and the other schools they'd played against. He'd have to work on building himself up.

He joined the B selection and slipped on one of the yellow bibs that Mr Carey had dumped on the ground. He introduced himself to the out-half, Paudie, and the scrum-half, Gav, but they just looked at him and shrugged. He wandered into position for the kick-off.

As the trial progressed, Eoin got more into the game, although Paudie didn't seem too interested in passing the ball to him so he had to seek it out for himself. The standard was a bit higher than Eoin was used to, but not so much that he felt out of place. He got a couple of chances to run, and got his passes away well too.

'Good display, Madden,' said Mr Carey at half-time. 'Switch with Woods and let's see what you can do at 10.'

Paudie Woods had a face like thunder when he passed Eoin. He leaned in to whisper in his ear, 'OK, kid, I want plenty of ball this half, and don't try anything smart.'

The A selection had led by 10 points at half-time, and extended that by another converted try early in the second. They were a comfortably better team than the Bs, as you would expect, but there were a few players on the second string who were trying hard to impress.

One of them was Gav, the scrum-half who seemed to be a mate of Paudie's, and who appeared to be having a dilemma. He didn't want Eoin to do well, but if he started throwing wild passes out to Eoin at out-half he himself would look bad, so he decided he'd let Paudie sort out his own problem.

Eoin hadn't seen much of the ball, and the game was rambling to an inevitable conclusion when Gav came up with one moment of brilliance, chipping the ball behind the As' defence and taking it beautifully on the bounce before hareing into the 22. He was taken down by the full-back but as he turned to release the ball, Eoin came charging up behind him and caught it cleanly, before he sidestepped the A team centre and dived in under the posts.

It was the only moment of magic in the whole game. Mr Carey seemed more enthused by it after the final whistle than by the comfortable win for the A team.

'Nice move, Gav! Well backed-up, Eoin,' grinned Devin, as they shook hands at the end. 'That'll give Mr Carey a few headaches!'

Chapter 6

· · · · · · · · ·

EOIN was happy with how he played – he was sure he had been better than Paudie Woods – but he found it less enjoyable than playing with his friends and knew he wouldn't be able to take charge of games in the way he used to. The Under 14s were struggling without him, and all their games seemed to clash with JCT training or matches.

The class bully, Richie Duffy, was furious that Eoin has been singled out for promotion as the star of the team – even though with Eoin gone it meant he could play out-half once again. But Eoin was more concerned that Rory and Dylan, particularly, were starting to resent his absence.

'Look, I'm sorry, guys!' he tried to explain as they lounged about in the doorway. 'I'm not too pushed about playing Js this year, but I can't say that to Carey. And it's just not in me to play badly.'

'But can't you just fake an injury and ask to play a few games on the 14s while you recover?' asked Rory.

'Will you listen to yourself?' laughed Eoin. 'How

could I be injured for one team and play on another?'

'Well …'

'Look, I'm probably not even going to get much chance to play so they might work out that it's better for me to get some game time on the 14s. But I'm not going to wimp out just because you guys think you need me.'

'Eoin's right,' said Alan. 'You're going to have stop complaining about it – it's like you're already writing the team off because Eoin's not playing. Sure you might as well give up rugby completely.'

'Well, I might,' grumbled Rory.

'Listen, I haven't played alongside Eoin since his very first game in sixth class,' Alan replied. 'But every week I go out and try to get better and maybe someday I'll get off the 3rds, and then maybe I'll burst through the 2nds onto the Js next year. That's the thing about rugby, about any sport – you've got to dream.'

The rest of the guys laughed at Alan, who was easily the worst player in the whole year.

'Ah, you're right, Al,' said Rory. 'It's just that it's not nearly as much crack when you're losing all the time.'

Dylan shrugged and looked at Eoin. 'What's the chances of me or Rory getting called up for that JCT squad?' he asked.

'I dunno.' Eoin replied, 'They have a couple of decent left-wingers, but I'd say Carey will keep his eye on you. The two guys who play scrum-half are excellent though. It will be hard to break in there ... sorry,' he told Rory.

'No need to apologise, I know who they are – and you're right,' Rory replied. 'My day will come.'

'Anyway, what else is happening? I'm getting bored with sleep-school-rugby-sleep,' said Eoin.

'Not much,' said Alan. 'Though I met Mr Finn and he was still talking about the trip to Belgium. He was wondering where you were going to bring us this year.'

Eoin groaned. 'Oh no, I hope he doesn't want us to enter the Young Historian again. It was great to win it, but there was too much stress involved. I've enough on my plate with the rugby too.'

'Fair enough, it's a huge amount of work. But he told me to tell you he would see you on Friday – he's bring-ing us out for the morning on a tour to Kilmainham Jail.'

'You'd better be careful they don't keep you, Dyl,' laughed Rory, who got a rugby boot in the shoulder for his trouble.

'Owww, that hurt,' whined Rory.

'Well keep your nasty digs to yourself then,' snarled Dylan as he stormed out. 'That wasn't funny.'

Eoin glared at Rory. 'What did you bring that up for? Dylan is NOT his father. He's a good lad and it's not his fault his father's in prison. Don't keep going on about it or you'll have to deal with dodging flying boots from me too.'

Chapter 7

. . . .

MR FINN had taught history for forty years at Castlerock, and he still helped out in his retirement. He was an old, great friend of Eoin's grandfather and had been very kind to Eoin in his first year at the school.

He stood at the top of the classroom where the boys were abuzz with the novelty of getting out of school for a few precious hours.

'OK, boys, settle down for a minute,' he started. 'I just want to tell you about the place we are visiting today. It's the famous old prison where the 1916 rebel leaders were executed, and you will see and hear a lot of interesting things about Irish history when you are there. I want you all on your best behaviour and to remember you are representing Castlerock.

'We will be leaving in the coach in ten minutes and it should take us no more than half an hour to get there. If anyone wants to use the bathroom, go now. And if any one of the rest of you has any questions, please ask them now.'

34

None of the boys were in a hurry to find out any more about Kilmainham Jail than was strictly necessary, so Mr Finn decided to fire a question back at them.

'OK, then, can anyone tell me which schools rugby player was executed in another prison on the north side of Dublin?'

He stared down at row after row of blank faces.

'A hint: he played for Belvedere.'

Still nothing.

'OK, one last hint, he had a famous song written about him.'

'Eh, was it Jesse James?' asked Pearse Hickey.

'No,' sighed Mr Finn. 'Although he wasn't executed in Kilmainham, I'm sure the tour guide could tell you all about this man if you tell him how interested you all are in rugby. Listen carefully, because you'll be studying this period for your exams next year.'

The bus ride across the city was slower than Mr Finn had expected. The traffic clogged up the streets and Eoin watched as cyclists, and even pedestrians, went sailing past.

They eventually reached the old prison, which hadn't held anyone since 1924. Its grey, grimy stone walls were anything but welcoming, and the carving over the main door of five snakes bound in chains signalled its old role as a place where wrong-doers would be locked out of the public's way.

Eoin's interest in history had been stoked by his contest win the previous year and he knew all about the decade of rebellion and bloodshed that led up to Irish independence. He had read about the 1916 Rising and was intrigued that they would be visiting where they rebels met their deaths.

The old prison was even less inviting inside than it had been on the outside, and the boys were glad they had worn their coats. The guide warned them to watch their step as the flagstones on the floor were uneven in places.

He also told them that Kilmainham was designed as a more modern, humane prison than the others at the time it was built, but Eoin couldn't imagine what they were thinking by installing such big barred windows. They might have allowed in more air and light, but they also let in more wind and rain, and there was a lot of that in Dublin.

'Grim place, isn't it?' said Dylan, staring at his feet.

'Yeah,' replied Eoin. 'I'd hate to spend even one night here.'

Dylan looked up at him. 'Yeah, can you imagine spending a few years locked up?'

Eoin looked at his pal and realised just what he was thinking; Dylan's father was in prison for serious crimes, one of which was the kidnap of Eoin and Caoimhe, Dylan's sister, at the previous year's schools' cup final.

'I'm sure modern prisons are a bit more comfortable. But I suppose losing your freedom must be terrible,' replied Eoin.

The boys followed at the back of the tour party, listening to tales of the prison's past. The tour finished outside in what the guide called the Stone Breakers' Yard. Surrounded by high, stone walls, in one corner stood a small, black cross. The guide led the boys over towards it, but kept a respectful distance.

'This is where the executions took place. In one week in May 1916, two or three each day, fourteen men were led here and shot.' He explained how one, James Connolly, had to be propped up in a chair due to his injuries and illness. And he explained how these weren't the only men whose lives had ended there.

Standing in the cold prison yard as the guide spoke to them really brought the history alive for the boys – Eoin felt he could almost imagine how it would have felt to stand, waiting for the firing squad … they looked at each other nervously.

'Capital punishment – the death penalty – was the

sentence for many crimes two hundred years ago, but we don't execute people any more in this country. During the various rebellions this was where many men spent their last night on earth, from the Fenians, to the War of Independence to the Civil War,' he told them.

'These boys play rugby in school,' Mr Finn told the guide. 'Could you tell them about another rugby player who was executed in those years, just a few miles up the road?'

'Of course, and I presume you mean Kevin Barry?' he replied. 'Kevin Barry was a medical student at UCD who took part in a raid on a bread van bringing supplies to the British Army in 1920. It went wrong and he was caught and executed in the gallows room in Mountjoy Jail.

'The most famous picture of him is of him wearing a rugby shirt – he went to Belvedere College.'

'Thank you very much,' said Mr Finn. 'That was a most informative tour and I'm sure it has stirred up even more interest in our history among the boys.'

The boys were quiet as they left – even Dylan wasn't chatting and jumping about; Irish history suddenly felt very recent and real to them all.

Chapter 8

∙ ∙ ∙ ∙ ∙ ∙ ∙ ∙ ∙

MR Carey came to the common room to tell Eoin that he had been picked on the replacements bench for the JCT's first friendly on Wednesday.

'We have to put in our panel of thirty-five with the Leinster branch next week and I'd like to be sure you are up to this,' he told him.

'Thank you, sir,' replied Eoin, still not sure whether he wanted to be part of the Junior Cup team at all.

Devin noticed the conversation and came over just as Mr Carey was leaving. He suggested to Eoin that they go out for a jog.

The pair ambled around the rugby pitch at a gentle pace, chatting about the games ahead and the great hopes Castlerock had for this year's Js.

'We haven't won it for years but this team has done well coming up and our main rivals, St Benedict's, have lost their two best players – emigrated to Australia, would you believe?'

'Ronan's really good,' Eoin said, about the Js' first-choice out-half.

'Yeah, he is,' said Devin, 'but he's an awful man for getting injured. He missed the Under 14s semi-final last year and we had to call up Paudie. He had a nightmare game and we were hammered.'

'Is Paudie in the squad for this game?'

'No, but I'd say we'll be picking three guys who can play out-half or centre so he won't be in the match-day 26, but he will be in the 35 we register with the branch. You should be ahead of him, so good luck if you get a run out.'

Two days later Eoin was standing around on the touchline, trying to keep warm, with just ten minutes left in the friendly. He had hoped he would get on at half-time, but it was Ronan's first match of the season and he needed to get some game-time under his belt.

Eventually, Mr Carey called over to the group of replacements. 'All right, you're all going on. Seven or eight minutes left, let's see what you can do.'

Eoin jogged on and took his position at out-half, the most important position on the team and from where all the big decisions are made. That fact came into his mind as he waited for play to resume.

Stay calm, just keep it simple, he thought to himself as play resumed with a line-out. *Just concentrate on not making any mistakes.*

The scrum-half, Paddy Buckley, flipped the ball back to Eoin, who ran three metres before being tackled and feeding it back neatly to the player following behind him. He sprang to his feet and got back in position as Castlerock's forwards started getting a maul going upfield. The game might have been over as a contest – Castlerock were twenty points up – but the replacements all wanted to make their mark.

The maul collapsed just inside the 22 and the backs lined up, ready to go on the attack. Paddy burrowed into the pile of bodies and fished out the ball. He paused, checking left and right, before scarpering off through a gap towards the line. Just as he crossed he was held up, and Eoin moved smartly to take the ball as it came back to him. With one fluid movement he dropped to the ground, aimed for the tiny amount of the try line that he could see, and squeezed the ball onto it.

'*Tweeeeeeeeep*,' went the whistle, and the referee raised his arm vertically.

'Nice one, Madden,' said Paddy, as they hauled themselves out of the heap and got their feet. 'You better kick it too,' he grinned.

Devin came up alongside, and explained that Eoin was the best kicker left on the field, and that he would be taking the conversion. 'Take it easy, it's a handy one but watch out for that wind,' he said.

Eoin took his time teeing up the ball, picking a few strands of grass and tossing them in the air to help gauge the wind speed and direction. Devin was right, there was quite a gale blowing.

He stepped back to his mark, then ran towards the ball, aiming away to the right. Almost as soon as he had hit the ball it was snatched by the wind and dragged back across the face of the goal. Incredibly, it hit the left hand goalpost with a clatter, fell like a stone and bounced again off the crossbar. Eoin blew out his cheeks, encouraging the ball over the bar, and sure enough, down it tumbled as the touch judges raised their flags.

'Ha! That was jammy,' grinned Devin as Eoin ran back, slightly embarrassed. 'Still, it worked!'

Eoin murmured 'thanks' as his team-mates chuckled their gratitude for his dramatic contribution, and he was relieved that the rest of the game passed without incident.

'Good work, Madden,' Mr Carey grunted, as he caught up with Eoin as he walked back to the accommodation block at the end of the game. 'You do the simple things very well and that's often forgotten by rugby players. I'll be sending your name off as one of our 35-man panel tomorrow. Congratulations, that doesn't happen very often to second years in this school.'

Chapter 9

. . . .

BACK in the dorm, trouble was brewing. Rory's smartphone had gone missing, and he was very angry.

'The door was locked, and the only people who have keys are you three and the housemaster's office. I'm going to go out for an hour and if it's not on my bed by the time I get back then I'm going to the headmaster,' he announced.

'Hang on, Rory, you don't think any of us took it, do you?' asked Eoin.

'I don't know,' said Rory, glowering at Eoin, Dylan and Alan in turn. 'Did you?'

He stormed out the door and Eoin stood, shocked, staring at the other two.

'That's mad,' he said. 'Does he not trust us?'

'Obviously not,' said Dylan. 'He probably thinks it was me because of my dad. He's never liked me, anyway.'

'Ah, stop that rubbish, Dyl. You had a few strops with him, but nothing serious. Sure aren't you two the stars of the Under 14s this year? He's just annoyed because it cost so much – I think he spent all his birthday money on it,' Eoin countered.

'Well, I'm not hanging around here either,' said Dylan, storming off up the corridor, leaving Eoin and Alan alone.

'If you nicked it I won't tell,' Alan whispered, looking across at Eoin with a serious face which broke into a grin after three seconds.

'I hope this gets sorted quickly,' Eoin muttered. 'This place won't be much fun if it doesn't turn up soon.'

Alan lay down on his bed and rooted around under his pillow. He sat up quickly, and threw the pillow aside.

'My phone!' he gasped.

Eoin stood up and walked across to Alan's bed. 'Is it missing too?'

Alan nodded.

'OK, let's have a good look around for it, it has to be here somewhere,' Eoin suggested.

They took all the sheets and blankets off the bed. Eoin crawled under it and searched around underneath. Alan took everything out of his locker and cleaned out his wardrobe and all the suitcases he had brought.

Nothing.

Eoin stood up, brushing the dust and chips of varnish off his hands.

'This is terrible,' he said. 'I don't think Dylan took anything but he's right that people will think that he did. I hope the phones turn up soon.'

'I can't stick around here,' said Alan. 'Let's go for a ramble.'

The pair headed off for a stroll around the grounds, and eventually ended up at the Rock, Eoin's favourite place in the whole school, which lay beside the bubbling stream.

'Oh, I forgot to tell you,' he started. 'I was here a couple of weeks ago and could swear someone was shooting at me.'

'Whaaaaaaat?' said Alan, stunned.

'Yeah, I know it sounds mad, but when I went off the first night I came down here for a while. I heard two bangs that I'd swear were gunshots – I think they came from the school.'

'Are you serious?' said Alan. 'That's no joke – you should have told McCaffrey.'

'I know. I know. But it seemed so stupid. And there was no harm done.'

'And what happens if they decide to shoot now – and they hit me? Then there's plenty of harm done. You need to report it.'

'OK,' muttered Eoin. 'I'll call in to him later.'

'Any word from Brian or Dave this year?' asked Alan. 'I'd love to see them as often as you can.'

Alan had discovered he too was able to see the ghosts that visited Eoin, but they had so far only appeared to him once.

'I don't know, it's a weird thing,' Eoin replied. 'Sometimes it seems I can call them up and other times they just appear when I really need them, but you just can't tell. There's something about this place here though. You can feel it's a bit spooky at times, especially in the evenings when the light is starting to go. I wonder was there anything on the site here long ago?'

'An ancient burial ground?' joked Alan. 'Maybe you could ask Mr Finn? He's writing a history of the school, isn't he?'

'Good idea, I'll have to be careful what I ask though.'

The boys turned to head back to their dorm, kicking a soft-drink can to each other as they dribbled across the field. Eoin suddenly felt a strange urge to turn around, and he stopped and looked back in the direction from which they had come. He saw a young man, dressed in a black and white rugby jersey, just standing at the entrance to the woods.

Eoin called out, 'Hey, are you lost?' but the man just turned and wandered back into the trees.

'I saw him! I saw him too!' said Alan. 'Is it a new ghost?'

'You're obsessed with seeing ghosts!' said Eoin, 'but I've no plans to head back down there after him. I wonder what's for tea?'

Chapter 10

· · · · · · · · · ·

HISTORY was the second class the next morning, and Alan gave Eoin an elbow in the ribs when Mr Finn came through the doorway.

'I'm afraid your history teacher, Mr Dunne, is sick today, so I'll be taking the class. What have you been studying recently?' he asked.

'The Easter Rising, sir,' replied Hugh Bowers.

'Ah, of course,' said Mr Finn. 'Sure weren't we all in Kilmainham last week. Does anyone remember the names of the leaders of the Rising?'

A couple of hands went up and the class got underway. Mr Finn was an inspirational teacher and soon had almost all the boys enraptured with stories from times gone by. He talked about the various flashpoints in the long search for Irish independence.

'Does anyone remember the name of the young man who was hanged in Mountjoy Jail – he was the one who played rugby?

'Barry, sir?' asked Daniel Reeves.

'Yes, that's right, Kevin Barry. I've been researching

the history of Castlerock and I had heard stories that he actually played against the school a year or two before he died. But I just haven't been able to find any evidence, which is very disappointing. However, I will bash on, as indeed you boys must do now – to the science laboratory, I believe.

Right on cue, the bell to end class came, and the boys left for their science class. Eoin hung back and cornered Mr Finn.

'Sir, can I ask you a question about Castlerock?'

'Of course, young Madden, fire away.'

'Well, do you know the little wood down by the stream? I just wondered what that was used for in the olden days. It has a strange atmosphere and I was wondering why it had been left as a wilderness when the rest of the school was used for buildings and playing fields.'

'That's a very good question, Eoin,' said Mr Finn. 'I confess I haven't a clue, but I'm working my way through the – sadly incomplete – school records and may find an answer to your query yet. Now run along, Mr Magee won't be happy if you're late for his class.'

Eoin tapped Dylan on the shoulder as they were leaving the last class that day.

'Fancy a run?' he asked. 'The Js are having a session

for forwards only so I'm off the hook.'

'Yeah, suppose so,' muttered Dylan, who hadn't been very communicative since the phones had gone missing. They went back to their dorm and quickly changed into tracksuits and trainers, locking the door as they went.

It was a bright, sunny autumn day and they enjoyed pushing themselves hard with sprints and chases through the fallen leaves. With the light closing in they finished off with a wind-down jog, which took them past the woods.

'You're always down here,' Dyl panted. 'What is it about it that brings you here so often?'

Eoin paused, not sure whether he wanted to bring another of his friends into his secret life on the edge of the spirit world. Alan hadn't been fazed by it at all but he was worried that Dylan might blab about it around the school – or think Eoin was going mad.

'Nothing really, I just like the atmosphere. It's perfect when you need a bit of peace.'

They stumbled through the glade to the Rock, and Eoin was startled to see a young man standing there, wearing a red, yellow and black hooped rugby jersey.

'What the ...?' gulped Dylan. 'Let's get out of here!'

'No, it's OK,' said Eoin. 'I know him. There's nothing to be afraid of.'

'Who is he?'

'That's Brian. I met him a couple of years ago. He was killed playing rugby—'

'Killed? So he's a ... a ghost?' Dylan whispered, looking rattled.

'Hello, Eoin,' said Brian. 'Had you a good summer? It was a bit boring for me, but I woke up this morning and found myself out here. Is there something going on at the school?'

Brian had been a great help to Eoin as he struggled to master the skills of rugby and the loneliness of boarding school life. He always seemed to crop up at the moments Eoin needed him most and Eoin thought of him almost like a big brother.

'Nothing major,' Eoin started.

'And who's your friend?'

'Dylan, Dylan Coonan,' Eoin replied, glancing at Dylan, who was staring at Brian with his mouth open.

'Yes, Dylan. You're the winger aren't you?' asked Brian.

'Yeah,' Dylan replied, nervously.

'Pleased to meet you,' said Brian, stretching out his arm before he pulled it back, realising Dylan could be a bit frightened by shaking the cold, dead hand of a ghost.

'What brought you to Castlerock?' Eoin asked.

'I'm not sure. There's something funny going on

though,' said Brian. 'I get a strong feeling that there's another spirit around the place.'

'That's weird. I was down here last night and saw another guy in a rugby shirt – it looked like a Belvo one. He didn't say anything and we didn't stick around.'

'Hmmm, there's something afoot I fear,' Brian muttered. 'I also found this beside the Rock,' he added, producing a brass bullet casing.

'That looks very old,' Eoin said, turning it in his hand. 'It must have been there for a long time.'

'I don't think so,' said Brian. 'It's still got its shine and I would have noticed it before. You hang on to it, Eoin. You might find out something about it.'

'We'd better be getting back,' said Dylan, clearly unnerved by the ghostly encounter.

'Alright, well if you hear anything you know where I'll be, Eoin,' said Brian. 'I don't have an awful lot else to do …'

Chapter 11

● ● ● ● ● ● ● ● ●

I T was a big Champions' League soccer night and most of the year was watching the match in the common room. Dylan still hadn't made up with Rory so they sat on opposite sides of the room.

Richie Duffy strolled in with his buddies and immediately noticed the strained seating arrangements.

'Heh, heh,' he sneered. 'So Baby Ror-ror and Baby Dyl-dyl are having a bit of a tiff … Hey Dylan, did you take away his soother – or was it something else?'

Dylan growled, but didn't rise to Duffy's jibes. Rory just looked away and pretended to concentrate totally on the football.

'Let's get out of here, Dyl,' said Eoin, who was tired and wanted to get back to the dorm. 'Don't mind that Duffy,' he continued as they left the room together, 'He's all wind. But were you a bit rattled by Brian earlier on?'

'Well … yeah …' said Dylan. 'But what really surprised me was that you seemed to know him well. What was that about?'

'Sorry, Dyl, I had to keep that from nearly everybody – you'd have thought I was mad. Brian has been around for a couple of years and has been a great help to me. He was the one that tipped off Alan about the kidnap at the Aviva last year – and saved me and Caoimhe.'

'Oh! … I always wondered about that,' Dylan admitted. 'I couldn't work out what Alan was doing in the car park so that he heard Caoimhe in the back. Still, I suppose I'd better thank Brian next time I see him.'

When they got back to their dorm, Eoin sat down on his bed and reached across to his locker. He slipped the key into the lock and turned it, reaching in behind the pile of books to where he had hidden his mobile.

But it wasn't there.

'Ah, no!' he said. 'My phone's gone! It was here just before we went out for the jog. And the door was locked!'

Dylan looked at him, and his face darkened. 'That's brutal, Eoin, but at least Rory can't blame me for stealing it.'

Eoin shrugged his shoulders, more concerned with losing the precious gift that Dixie had given him the year before.

Alan and Rory arrived at the door, and Dylan filled them in: 'Eoin's phone has been nicked. We locked the door and went out for a jog – together – and when we came back it was gone. So it can't have been me…'

He slipped past the others and walked off down the corridor.

'I told you it couldn't have been him,' said Eoin. 'He's a good guy and doesn't need you to be at him about his dad. Even if you don't say it, he knows where you're coming from.'

Rory shrugged and wandered off in the opposite direction to Dylan.

'We should go to see Mr McCaffrey,' Alan said to Eoin.

The Castlerock headmaster was in his office when the boys knocked at the door.

'Come in. Ah, Madden and Handy, how can I help you?'

Eoin explained what had happened, and how he was concerned that Dylan would be blamed for the missing phones.

'I was with him all the time when mine was stolen, and I'm sure he wouldn't have taken the other ones, sir. But Rory has jumped to conclusions and I'm afraid it could get around the school.'

Mr McCaffrey sat back in his chair and tapped his pencil off the desk.

'Well, of course we will do our best to ensure that

doesn't happen. But we also must try to get your property back. Now show me where you are sleeping this year.'

The boys led Mr McCaffrey back up to their dorm where he made them stand by the door while he searched for the phone. When he couldn't find it, he took his own mobile out and asked Alan what his number was, and then dialled it.

'Ssssh,' he went. The trio strained their ears to try to hear anything. And sure enough, there was a muffled '*dring dring; dring dring*' sound coming from somewhere under the bed.

Mr McCaffrey laughed. 'You just need to look a bit harder, boys. It seems like the great Headmaster Sherlock has solved another mystery.'

He turned and left, chuckling to himself as he wandered down the corridor.

Eoin ducked under the bed, but still couldn't see any sign of a phone. Alan joined him and at once noticed what had changed.

'That's weird,' he said. 'I was down under here the first night and noticed this trapdoor, but it was sealed shut. Look how the varnish has cracked around it. Someone has opened it recently.'

Chapter 12

. . . .

ALAN tried to work his fingers around the edges of the trapdoor, but it remained tightly shut.

'You can probably push it open from the other side,' he said. 'That must be where the thief's been coming from.'

'Let's move the leg of the bed on top of it,' suggested Eoin. 'That would slow him down a fair bit, whoever he is.'

'Our phones are still down there though – we need to get them back.'

'OK, I wonder does Mr Finn know anything about secret passageways?'

They wandered down to the staff common room and knocked on the door. Mr Carey answered it, listened to their request and told them to wait outside. Boys never got to cross the threshold of that room.

'What can I do to help you?' asked Mr Finn.

'Sir, remember you said you were writing about the school's history? Well, have you ever heard of a secret passage?' asked Eoin.

'Well ... not really,' Mr Finn answered cautiously. 'Why do you ask?'

'I think someone has been getting into our room through a trapdoor in the floor – and they've been stealing mobile phones!' answered Eoin.

'That's very interesting,' the old teacher replied. 'I heard rumours about such a passage back when I was a student here, but no-one I know had ever found it and it doesn't appear on the original plans for the college, which I have been examining recently. You must show me this trapdoor.'

The boys brought Mr Finn upstairs and lifted the bed off the mysterious doorway cut into the wooden floor.

'Very wise. I'd keep that bed on top of it until we get to the bottom of this.'

He checked where the room was in the building and spent some time looking up and down the corridor outside.

'Very mysterious,' he said. 'I will have to study this further. Don't mention it to any other pupils. We don't want them going off on a hunt for the culprit or his hiding place.'

Eoin was annoyed to lose his mobile, but Dylan let him text his mum to tell her, so she wouldn't worry when he didn't answer. With the schoolwork piling on and rugby training eating into every spare hour, he soon forgot about it. He was an unused replacement for the Js' next two friendlies and was starting to feel a bit rusty.

'I wish Carey would allow me to play with you guys,' he told Rory in the dorm one evening. 'I won't be much use in an emergency if I haven't played a game for weeks. I've had less than ten minutes on the pitch all season!'

'I'll ask him can you turn out on Saturday morning – we're going down to play Rostipp in Tipperary and you could visit your folks,' Rory replied.

'Do you think he'd let me?' Eoin wondered, 'The Js don't have a game and I'd love to get out of the school – and those training sessions – even for a day,.'

Rory was a skilled talker and Mr Carey proved more co-operative than Eoin expected. On Saturday morning he, Rory and Dylan got up early to join the rest of the Under 14s for the two-hour trip down the country. They were first on the coach and took the prime positions down the back. Eoin was tired and just wanted to doze off, but he was interrupted by Richie Duffy, shadowed as usual by his sidekicks Flanagan and Sugrue.

'Ah, you're back slumming it with us now, eh, Madden?' Richie sneered. 'Dropped off the JCT already.'

'No, just back to show you how a real out-half plays,'

Eoin shot back.

Duffy's face turned white. 'But, but …' he started, before walking up to the top of the bus where Mr Hoey was sitting alongside Mr Finn.

'Who's playing out-half today?' Duffy asked the teacher.

Mr Hoey looked up from his crossword and stared at the boy.

'Well, for a start, you need to address me as "sir", and then you need to say "excuse me",' the teacher replied. 'Then you need to go back to your seat while the bus is in motion. I'll be having a discussion with the captain, Charlie Johnston, before we arrive in Rostipp. You will be informed in due course.'

Duffy walked back to his seat with his face like thunder. The rest of the team had heard Mr Hoey's lecture and most of them were amused at Duffy's discomfort.

Charlie turned in his seat and caught Eoin's eye at the back of the bus, and gave him an exaggerated wink.

Chapter 13

. . . .

ROSTIPP was only a twenty-minute drive from Ormondstown so Eoin wasn't surprised that his mum, dad and grandfather had come out to see him play. They had brought Dylan's mum too, and his sister Caoimhe, who gave the boys a big wave as they trotted out onto the pitch in the green and white hoops of Castlerock.

Eoin was selected to play at out-half, much to Richie Duffy's disgust, and he settled into his favourite position without any fuss.

Although both teams were just a year younger than the players he had been training with this year, they seemed so much smaller, and judging by the way they threw the ball around in the warm-up, less skilled. Eoin felt that he had moved up several steps on the rugby ladder.

That wasn't to say it was much easier – the big, bruising Savage brothers from his home town of Ormondstown made sure of that.

'I hear you're a bit of a rugby star up at Castlerock,'

George said as the teams lined up for the kick-off.

'Well, you'll be seeing stars by the time we're finished with you,' added his brother Roger.

Eoin laughed and hoofed the ball high into the air where it hung momentarily before Charlie Johnston caught it and the ruck formed around him.

Castlerock were a bit of a shambles in the first half, but Eoin kept them in it with his kicking and they changed ends 10-6 down.

'We need more ball in the backs, Madden,' Duffy complained as they sucked their slices of orange.

'OK, hold it there please,' Mr Hoey chipped in. 'I have a few plans of my own and I'll be obliged if you listen to me instead.'

Eoin listened to the coach, who had some good ideas on what needed to be done. As the players moved away to restart the half, Mr Hoey took Eoin aside.

'Look, you're our best player by far and you're kicking well. But their backs look vulnerable so I'd like you to give ours a chance to expose them now and again.'

Eoin nodded, realising that his dislike for Duffy might be clouding his judgement and preventing him from giving him the ball.

He got a chance to atone early in the second half, but Duffy was too slow to the pass and knocked the ball forward.

'Come on, Duffy!' roared Charlie. 'Keep your eye on what's going on.'

Duffy glowered at Eoin, who shrugged back at him.

The next time Eoin had the ball in his hand he flung an inch-perfect pass to Duffy, but the inside-centre hesitated in deciding what to do next and was soon swarmed by the Rostipp forwards.

Eoin put over a tricky penalty goal, but with less than five minutes left Castlerock were 13-9 down.

'Come on, Castlerock!' came the high-pitched call from the touchline, and Eoin grinned at Dylan as his sister waved a home-made banner.

From the next line-out Eoin gathered the ball and, spotting a gap, decided to make a run through midfield. He rode a tackle and was only ten metres from the try-line when one of the Savage brothers came crashing in from his left. As he fell he twisted and spotted two team-mates chasing hard in support: Duffy to his left, Dylan to his right.

'Pass!' roared Duffy, but Eoin slipped the ball to Dylan who was very fast over short distances and nipped over the line and touched down under the posts.

'Hooray!' shrieked Caoimhe, and the rest of the Castlerock supporters joined in with her celebrations.

Eoin knocked over the conversion and with a three-point lead Castlerock concentrated on closing the game down for the last couple of minutes. At the final whistle he shook hands with the Rostipp boys and his team-mates and walked over to where his family were standing.

'Well done, son,' his father said, clapping him across the shoulders. His mum and grandad also congratulated him, and both slipped him some pocket money.

'Any sign of your phone?' his mother asked.

'Not yet, but I hope we'll get them back soon,' replied Eoin.

A loud whistle called him back to the field where Mr Hoey wanted to have a warm-down and short discussion on how they had played.

Duffy continued to give Eoin daggers, but Mr Hoey was full of praise for Eoin's late burst and the quick decision that saw him pass the ball to Dylan.

'You'll be back at out-half next week, Mr Duffy,' he said, 'but we need the sort of speedy decision-making that Mr Madden showed today from now on. Now, get yourselves changed and we'll be back on the bus in twenty minutes.'

Eoin hurried over for a quick farewell to his family, and also thanked Caoimhe and Dylan's mum for their vocal support.

'See you at Hallowe'en, Caoimhe,' he called out as he was leaving. 'What are you dressing up as?'

'She doesn't need to dress up!' laughed Dylan, as they clambered onto the bus.

Chapter 14

. . . .

THE trip down the country had heartened Eoin. Although he enjoyed life in Castlerock, still missed his mam and dad, and his grandfather, of course.

Back at school the history teacher, Mr Dunne, had informed them that even though it was fantastic that Eoin had won the Historian of the Year competition the previous year, there just wasn't enough time in the school timetable to defend his title. Eoin was secretly happy; he had worked very hard on the project, but he knew the reason he had won was the advantage he had been given by his ghostly friend Dave Gallaher.

Mr Dunne wasn't letting them totally off the hook, however, as a project was part of the preparation for the state exams and he expected them all to come up with a strong topic by the next History class.

He collared Eoin as the class broke up.

'I know you're busy with rugby and everything else, Eoin,' the teacher started, 'But you really have a talent for history and I'd like you to spend a bit of time working out a good topic. You could be in line for an A next year if you get the right idea for a project. See what you come across and we'll talk next week.'

It was a warm day so after school Eoin and Alan went for a ramble down to the woods. Eoin told Alan how Dylan had also been able to see Brian, but was a bit rattled by the experience.

Alan laughed. 'I wish I could see Brian more often. He seemed like such a nice lad. And knowing a ghost is so cool …'

They stepped into the bushes and walked past where the stream flowed, where they saw someone digging at the base of the Rock.

'Hello?' Eoin started.

The young man stood up, and Eoin realised he had seen him some weeks before. Up close he recognised the Belvedere College rugby jersey that he was wearing.

'Excuse me,' the young man said, 'I didn't hear you coming. I recognise you from somewhere, don't I?'

Eoin shrugged, 'I don't know how, my name is Eoin Madden, and this is Alan Handy. Who are you?'

'I'm sorry, of course I should have introduced myself. My name is Kevin, Kevin Barry …' he replied.

Eoin and Alan's eyes widened.

'*The* Kevin Barry?' Eoin interrupted. 'We went to Kilmainham Jail a few weeks ago… The tour guide told us all about your execution.'

'Yeah, our teacher even sang a ballad about you on the bus back afterwards,' said Alan.

'I remember now,' started Kevin. 'I'm often up there too seeing some old comrades, and I was in that yard when you guys were being taken around – I remember Alan here acting the maggot – and heard the old teacher mention my name. I didn't think anyone knew much about me anymore, except for that terrible song I keep hearing ...'

'What's brought you to Castlerock,' Eoin asked, 'Was it because you saw us at Kilmainham?'

'I'm not sure. There's something going on, though. I saw another ghost here last night too. He told me that he only appears here when there's a problem ...'

'That would be Brian,' said Eoin. 'He was killed playing rugby at Lansdowne Road.'

'I remember playing at Lansdowne Road. I think I played rugby here once for Belvedere – we hammered you if memory serves me correct.'

'Ha, well that wouldn't happen anymore!' Eoin grinned.

'Do Belvo still play?' asked Kevin.

'Yeah, they do,' replied Alan. 'They're not bad, but even Castlerock would expect to beat them and we've won nothing in years.'

Eoin stared at the new arrival. He was perplexed by the arrival of a third ghost at the school. *Why me?* he thought.

'Has anyone else been able to see you since you died?' asked Alan.

'No ... I don't think so,' replied Kevin. 'It's hard to know, because sometimes I see people staring at me, but they never approach me. I was always a bit shy too, and I'm not mad on talking about the whole "being dead" thing.'

'I don't really understand the ghost thing either,' said Eoin. 'You're the third I've met in about two years and no-one else was able to see them. But now Alan can see ghosts if he's with me.'

'Maybe it's because there was a crisis when I saw Brian for the first time?' asked Alan. 'Maybe Kevin here is going to solve the mystery of the thefts?'

'Hold up there, please,' said Kevin. 'I'm no detective, I'm just a long-dead medical student. I'm no good at all at mysteries.'

'All right,' grinned Eoin, 'don't worry about that. I don't want to even start explaining mobile phones to you!'

The trio sat chatting about school and rugby for a

while, before Eoin had a brainwave.

'Would you mind if I interviewed you about your life?' he asked Kevin. 'We have a big project to do in history class and you would be perfect.'

'So I'm a part of history now?' sighed Kevin.

'Yes, kids in school are taught about you. Don't you know that?'

'No, I didn't. But I suppose that's nice, really. I just did my bit. It wasn't much.'

'I really would like to find out more about you. Please?'

'Well, alright then. Bring your ink-pen and jotter down here tomorrow and we can talk.'

'Eh … "ink-pen"? I think you've got a lot to learn about modern schools! OK then, I'll see you tomorrow.'

Kevin disappeared and Eoin and Alan wandered back to the dorm.

'Smart idea, Eoin,' Alan said. 'Sorry I didn't think of it first.'

'Yeah, well that's why I'm Young Historian of the Year and you're not,' he laughed, turning up the pace and leaving Alan behind as he raced up the staircase.

Chapter 15

· · · · · · · · · ·

THE Junior Cup team's first game was against St Osgur's, and Eoin took his place on the touch-line in Donnybrook. These games always drew a large crowd both of pupils and past pupils of the schools, heaping even more pressure on the players.

That wasn't something that concerned Eoin, who had kept his nerve to kick a last-second conversion in front of an almost-full Aviva Stadium to win the Father Geoghegan Cup. That had been an amazing experience, which capped his first year at Castlerock – and his first playing rugby.

It was different now – he was acknowledged as a very good player and his promotion to the JCT squad was recognition of this.

The teams lined up for press photographs, and as they broke up Eoin gave a wave to his classmates as they fooled around in various green and white outfits, carrying banners proclaiming the greatness of Castlerock.

The players certainly showed it on the field, romping to a 24-0 lead at half-time.

'That was good work, lads,' Mr Carey said at the break. 'We are in good control up front, and the backs have kept everything simple. I want to empty the bench over the second half, to give you all a taste of a big crowd, but I won't do anything till the last twenty minutes. Keep doing what you're doing and try to build on that lead.'

The second row, JD Muldowney, scored two tries for Castlerock and widened the margin between them and St Osgur's, and Mr Carey brought on four new forwards half-way through the second period. He nodded to Eoin and the rest of the replacements, and opened his hand wide to show them they would be on in five minutes.

Eoin kept his focus on the game, afraid to even think about his nerves, just preparing for his call-up.

'Right, Madden, Touhy, Gillespie, warm up there. You're on at the next break in play.'

Eoin did a series of short sprints up the touchline, ignoring the calls of encouragement and banter that were coming from his pals, and when Mr Carey signalled them to go on, he went straight to his position.

'No special instructions from coach then?' asked Devin.

'No, he just said "keep it tight and keep the scoreline blank",' replied Eoin.

Castlerock's forwards were much bigger and stronger than their opponents and every scrum, line-out, ruck or maul was a walkover. Eoin got a few passes and kicked them all upfield where the forwards were soon feeding them back once again.

Into the last minute the lead had mounted to 39-0 when JD knocked the ball on and the St Osgur's scrum-half gathered and galloped upfield. Eoin was quickest off in pursuit and by the time he had crossed the Castlerock 22 he was on the No.9's shoulder. The Osgur's player looked behind him and the sight of Eoin right in his tracks seemed to rattle him into a moment's hesitation. Eoin struck ten metres from the line, a flying tackle knocking the player and sending the ball spilling out of his hands and rolling end-over-end across the dead ball line.

Eoin helped the St Osgur's scrum-half to his feet as the referee blew the final whistle. 'Sorry about that,' he grinned sheepishly.

'Ah, sure we were well outclassed,' came the reply. 'We didn't really deserve a consolation try.'

The Castlerock fans cheered as the teams came off, and Mr Carey had a rare, broad grin across his face.

'Superb stuff, men,' he said. 'That was a very efficient performance and you deserve to have won by that margin. Now, we're in the quarter-finals and every game from now on will be a lot harder. So let's see you all for a light run–out tomorrow after school and we'll discuss what we can do better.'

Later that evening, Eoin lay down on his bed, staring at the ceiling until his eyes started to feel heavy. The term was flying past, and he had trained almost every day. He felt really fit, but also needed more sleep than usual.

'Eoin …' came a hesitant voice. 'Are you awake?'

Eoin opened his eyes, and was a little startled to see Brian standing at the end of his bed. Brian had never come into the school before, besides one visit to the library.

'Brian, what are you doing here?'

'Sorry, Eoin. A voice came to me telling me to talk to you as soon as possible. I hope you don't mind me visiting you here.'

'It's OK, but what have you to tell me?'

'I'm not even sure what it means,' Brian replied. 'But the message was "get someone to twist the rose on the fireplace as you push down on the opposite corners of the trapdoor". Does that make any sense to you?'

Eoin asked Brian to repeat the instructions before he explained about the trapdoor and the stolen phones.

Brian was surprisingly up-to-date on mobile telephones, having spent most of the time since his death at the stadium on Lansdowne Road, where he saw the changing fashions and advancing technologies over the best part of a century.

'Thanks, Brian.' said Eoin, 'I'd better wait till the lads get back before I try that. By the way I hear you've met the other ghost, Kevin?'

'Yes, and quite a surprise it was to me. He's a nice lad but there's a bit of a mystery about him ... I think he's looking for something down at the Rock.'

Chapter 16

· · · · · · · · · ·

ALAN and Dylan came up to the dorm soon after Brian had left, and Eoin explained his mysterious message.

'You really seem to have some serious connections with the ghostly world, Eoin,' said Alan. 'Someone's trying to help us.'

There was a black iron rose in the middle of the old, blocked-up fireplace, and Alan gripped hold of it as the other pair clambered under the bed.

'Now,' called Eoin as he and Dylan pushed down at the corners of the trapdoor. The rose was stuck, and needed some serious effort by Alan, but he soon worked it loose and a noisy mechanism cranked into life behind the walls.

The trapdoor felt loose under Eoin's hand. He pushed hard until the corner came free and he and Dylan got their hands underneath it. They pushed the heavy trapdoor aside and stared down into the hole.

'Has anyone got a torch?' Eoin called, and Alan brought him the bicycle lamp he used for late-night reading.

Eoin paused, shining the light down and spotting that a short staircase led up to the opening. He looked at his friends, grinned nervously, and said, 'Here goes.'

Down he stepped, sweeping the lamp from left to right as he went. At the bottom he called to his friends who followed him down, first Dylan and then Alan. They shone the lamp around as their eyes got used to the darkness. On the left hand wall stood a doorway with a bolt across it, sealed with a huge lock. On the right was another door which appeared to be ajar.

'Do you want to go in there?' asked Eoin.

'Yeah, let's see where it leads,' replied Dylan.

'Hang on, guys, just wait a second. We heard the phones down here – shouldn't we look for them first?' suggested Alan.

Eoin flashed the light around, taking care to light up every corner of the room and, sure enough, the three stolen mobiles were sitting on a small bench against the far wall.

'Hang on,' said Dylan. 'We shouldn't touch them yet – then the thieves will know we've been here. They don't seem to want them immediately; maybe we should leave them here until the teachers come.'

'Good thinking,' said Alan.

Eoin turned to the open door and slipped through

without touching the handle. He found himself in a corridor, and about fifteen metres away he spotted a ladder. He showed it to his pals, holding his index finger to his lips to show them he wanted them to be silent, and started up the ladder.

He stopped at the top where he found another trap-door, and listened. There was a muffled sound of talking and laughing, and the edges of the opening leaked light.

He carefully went back down the ladder, again motioning to Alan and Dylan to stay quiet, and led them back along the corridor. He counted his paces as he went, and finished at the foot of the staircase to their own dorm.

'23, 24, 25 … 26,' he finished.

'What was that about?' asked Dylan.

'He's counting the steps from our room to whoever else has been using the passageway,' said Alan. 'If he counts twenty-six steps out the door of our dorm he'll be outside their door.'

'Exactly,' grinned Eoin. 'Now what do you want to do about the phone, Alan? I'm inclined to agree with Dyl and leave it there for the moment.'

Alan went along with the plan and the trio climbed back into their bedroom. Without a second's delay, Eoin began counting again, strode out the door and turned left down the corridor. He went silent as he neared the end of his sequence, and mouthed '26' to his friends as he stopped right outside the door to dormitory number 11.

Alan's eyes widened as Dylan's face darkened.

The trio turned on their heels and went back to their dorm, closing the door firmly behind them.

They looked at each other, wary of what would happen next.

Alan was first to speak the word they all had at the front of their minds. 'Duffy!'

Chapter 17

• • • • • • • • •

'**N**OT just Duffy,' said Dylan, 'but Sugrue, Flanagan and Humphries as well.'

'We'd better make sure we're completely right on this, lads,' said Eoin. 'That gang will destroy us if we slip up. We need to get the teachers in on this as soon as possible.'

'But McCaffrey and Duffy's father are best friends,' whined Alan. 'He's always going on about how much fund-raising he does for the school. He won't do anything to him.'

'OK,' said Eoin, 'here's what we do. We show Mr Carcy and Mr Finn what we found. They'll be horrified and won't allow it to be hushed up.'

'I wonder what's behind the other door?' asked Alan.

'That lock looked pretty solid,' said Dylan.

'Look, the sooner this is sorted and we get our phones back the better,' said Eoin. 'I'll go down to the staff room now.'

Dylan went along too, and Alan stayed behind to keep an eye on the secret chamber.

Mr Finn was talking to Mr Carey outside the staff room. He hailed Eoin as he came down the stairs.

'Ah, Master Madden, hero of the JCT I hear.'

Eoin blushed because Mr Carey was present, and mumbled his thanks.

'I'm sorry to interrupt, sirs, but we've discovered something serious in our room. Can you come up with us?'

The teachers immediately looked concerned, but Eoin assured them it wasn't anything dangerous. Or at least he hoped it wasn't.

When they got to the room he explained how three mobiles had gone missing, and how they had heard the sound of them ringing – he left out Mr McCaffrey's part in their discovery – and how they had found the trapdoor. He also explained how they found their way in – leaving out the part about Brian – and showed the teachers the staircase.

Alan handed Mr Carey his lamp and the rugby coach led the way down.

'We didn't touch the phones, sir, in case you need to fingerprint them or something?' said Dylan.

Mr Carey came back up through the floor a few minutes later. He dropped the mobiles on the bed.

'I presume you discovered the ladder at the end of

the corridor. Do you happen to know where it leads?' he asked.

'Yes sir,' replied Eoin. 'It's No.11. Duffy, Sugrue ...'

Mr Carey looked at Mr Finn. 'This is very disturbing ...' Mr Finn started.

'Don't worry about fingerprints or any of that,' Mr Carey chipped in. 'Just be happy you got your phones back.'

'But, sir—' started Eoin.

'I'll have a word with the occupants of room 11, and be assured this will not happen again.'

And with that the teachers left.

'That's really annoying,' said Alan.

'They're going to let them away with it,' said Dylan.

Eoin stopped and looked at his two room-mates. 'There's something that just doesn't add up,' he said. 'Why did Duffy's gang leave the phones down there?'

'They just wanted to cause trouble and they knew Rory would blame me,' said Dylan.

'Maybe,' said Eoin. 'But why haven't they gone back down there? There's something missing here and I'm going to try to find out what it is.'

'How are you going to do that?' asked Alan.

'I don't know,' he replied, slipping into a hoody, 'but one of the spooks might have an idea.'

Eoin brought a notebook and pen down to the Rock, as he needed to get moving on that history project. He was glad to see that Kevin was there, again scrabbling round at the base of the enormous stone.

'Hello, Kevin,' announced Eoin. 'I wonder is this a good time to start that interview?'

Kevin nodded, and stood up, stretching his ghostly bones. 'No time like the present,' he laughed. 'Especially when all you have is a past.'

He explained to Eoin about his days as a boy living in the countryside of County Carlow, and how his family moved to Dublin where his father worked on his dairy in Fleet Street in the city centre.

He talked too about his schooldays, first out in Rathmines at St Mary's College and, when that school closed down, in Belvedere College which was a short walk from his home.

'I used to ramble up Sackville Street – I think they call it O'Connell Street now – past the GPO and up to the school. Dublin was a different place then, very few motor cars and nearly everyone wore a cap.

'It all changed for me after the Easter Rising in 1916. I thought those men were very brave and I joined up after that. Here, take a look at this – my souvenir of the rebellion …'

Kevin poked around in his pocket but looked confused when he couldn't find what he was looking for.

'That's very annoying. For years I've been carrying around a bullet case that I found up on Sackville Street …'

'Is this what you were looking for?' asked Eoin, producing the bullet he and Brian had found weeks before. 'I found it down here.'

'It is indeed!' chirped Kevin, delighted to see his keepsake once again. 'I went up to the GPO when it was all over …The place was covered in rubble. My mother was very annoyed when she found out I'd been up there – I suppose I was about your age, Eoin. Just gone fourteen.'

'And was it scary?' asked Eoin.

'No, there were lots of soldiers around but the place was such a mess no-one paid any heed to me. I found lots of these things,' he said, pointing to the bullet casing, 'and swapped them with my pals for cigarette cards and toffees. I kept one to remind me of the rebels though.'

A few raindrops started to fall, but within seconds there was a steady strumming on the leaves as the rain got heavier.

Eoin went to hide under a tree, but his new friend just grinned.

'Not much point me worrying about getting a chill, is there?' Kevin laughed. 'Mind yourself there,' he said as he pulled the thicker leaves over where Eoin was standing. 'Remind me of a day when I ran home all the way from Rathmines using a rhubarb stick and leaf as an umbrella. The passers-by all thought I was mad.'

Eoin laughed too, as Kevin mimed his attempt to avoid the raindrops.

'I'd better be heading back,' Eoin said, pulling on his hood, 'But it would be great if you could ask Brian to get in touch with me when he's next around.'

Chapter 18

· · · · · · · · · ·

EOIN got soaked running across the playing fields back to the dormitory, and when he woke next morning he found he was starting to sniffle. By lunch-time he was sneezing and Mr McCaffrey sent him to see the nurse, Miss O'Dea, who told him to go back to bed.

'Take this lemon and honey drink with you and try to sleep,' she told him. 'I'll call up to see you about four o'clock. What classes do you have this afternoon? I'll tell the teachers.'

Eoin listed off the subjects he would be missing, but remembered something else. 'Oh, Miss, can you tell Mr Carey too, he'll expect me at the JCT training. We have a big game tomorrow,' he said.

'Tomorrow? I don't think you'll be well enough in time to play tomorrow,' she told him. 'But I'll let Mr Carey know.'

Eoin was miserable enough without missing the big rugby match too. Why were the days you were allowed to stay in bed always the days you felt too terrible to enjoy it?

He dozed off eventually, but was awoken by a rustling noise in the corner. He opened one eye to see Brian peering under Alan's bed where the trapdoor lay.

'Hey, Brian,' he said, 'what are you doing here?'

'Kevin told me you wanted to see me,' he replied. 'And I was wondering about that trapdoor message – I presume the trapdoor is the one under this bed?'

'Yes,' said Eoin. 'It leads to a secret passageway that goes up to another dorm. The lads in there were using it to sneak in here and steal our phones. It was weird, though, they just took the phones out of here and then left them down in the secret room. We told the teachers, but they don't seem too interested in finding out any more about who did it or why. There's a second door down there too, with a huge lock on it. It's all very mysterious.'

'I'll have a look around. Why are you in bed during the daytime?'

'I woke up with a cold this morning. The nurse says I can't play in the Junior Cup quarter-final tomorrow, which is a pain.'

'Well, she's probably right. Never a good idea to play a match too soon after a cold. I've seen a lot of lads get much worse. Get yourself right for the semi. They'll be fine without you.'

Brian was right, of course, and Eoin was still in bed when Castlerock found their way past St Ultan's in the quarter-final. Rory came straight up to the room to give him a blow-by-blow account of the game.

'It was too close for Carey to empty the bench, so Paudie never got a look-in,' he chuckled. 'He wasn't too happy about that. Paddy Buckley got a knock though, so Gav got on. I suppose I've moved up in the scrum-half pecking order too ...' he added.

'You definitely have,' said Eoin. 'But I think they can only play guys in the 35 they send in before the cup starts.'

'Oh,' said Rory, suddenly gutted.

'Sorry to break that to you, pal. It's just the stupid rules.'

'But what if ...' he started, before shrugging his shoulders and sighing. 'Oh well, there's always next year. We've a decent team – or we will when we get you back anyway.'

Dylan and Alan arrived, and the four sat around talking rugby for a while before Dylan tried out one of his stupid jokes and they all cracked up laughing.

'Thanks for coming to visit me, lads,' chuckled Eoin. 'Just a shame no one cared enough to bring me a few grapes.'

Chapter 19

• • • • • • • • • •

EOIN recovered quickly and a couple of days after the JCT game he was up and about. His return to training took a couple of days more.

'OK, Eoin, good to have you back,' Devin called as he jogged onto the training pitch. 'How are you feeling?'

'Good, thanks,' he replied. 'Raring to go.'

'Right, Ronan's looking a bit dodgy for the semi,' said the captain. 'I want you to work with the first team backs in case you need to be brought in. Mr Carey's still not sure whether to stick with Paudie, but I'm pulling hard for you.'

Eoin nodded and took his place with the backs. The session went well, but when it came to rejigging the first team backline, Mr Carey called out KPaudie Woods's name.

'OK, Woods, let's see what you can do with the big boys,' he called, as Eoin gritted his teeth. Devin looked across and shrugged, as if to say that he had done his best, but the teacher had made the final call.

Paudie did OK too, but Eoin still reckoned he was a

better out-half. Paudie was just too slow making decisions and was often caught in possession. Eoin knew whether a pass or a kick was the better option before the scrum-half had even turned to pass him the ball. He wished he had another chance to show that to Mr Carey.

Eoin was put at full back and made a couple of tackles and one good catch under a garryowen, but that was all he saw of the play in twenty minutes on the field.

Devin sought him out after training, laying his arm across Eoin's shoulder and telling him to stay focused, that his time was coming.

'Thanks,' Eoin shrugged, 'but I'd probably be better off playing the rest of the season on the 14s.'

'No you wouldn't,' insisted Devin. 'This is a lot tougher, better training, more competitive games. You don't realise it now, but you're becoming a better player every day. Stick at it, you'll get your chance. I'm certain of it.'

The following weekend Eoin and Dylan went home to Ormondstown. Because they had both turned fourteen their parents decided they could travel on the bus, as long as they stayed together. It was quite an adventure for the pair – their new independence was very exciting.

'Any plans for the weekend?' Dylan asked.

'Eat, sleep and watch some TV that doesn't involve sharing the remote with sixty other people,' Eoin laughed.

'Yeah, I'm wrecked. Need some home cooking and nothing much else. Catch you around the town maybe?'

'Yeah, maybe a bag of chips tomorrow, say six o'clock?'

Eoin's dad was there at the bus-stop, and he dropped Dylan home too. Caoimhe waved at them from the window.

Eoin had the lazy weekend he had hoped for, tucking into shepherd's pie and roast beef and enjoying the simple pleasures of being home with his mum and dad. He called around to see Dixie, too, and naturally asked his grandfather had he heard of Kevin Barry.

'Sure I did, indeed. Your grandmother used to sing a ballad about him. "Just a lad of eighteen summers..."' he sang.

'I'm doing a project about him,' Eoin said. 'And as you were so useful last year...'

'Ha! Now, don't say that. Your hard work won that competition for you. But to be honest, I don't know much about him. He played a bit of rugby, didn't he?'

'Yes, for Belvo,' Eoin replied. 'He was from Carlow originally.'

'Ah, yes.' said Dixie, 'I met a man once who knew him from down there. Said he was a quiet fellow, a serious type.'

'Still is,' said Eoin, before he realised what he had said.

Dixie looked at Eoin strangely.

'I mean, I mean … he still *was* when he was up in Dublin,' said Eoin. 'I found a book about him that said that too.'

'Well, that book should help you write your project then,' said Dixie. 'They were terrible times he lived through. He wouldn't have been much older than yourself when he joined the rebels. Some people thought Ireland wouldn't win its independence without a fight, others preferred to do it through politics. In the end it took a bit of both, but it took many years to heal the scars of those times. A lot of mothers buried their sons – on all sides.'

Eoin told his grandad about the rugby season so far, and how he had spent more time watching the games than playing in them.

'It's funny,' said his grandad, 'when I played there was no such thing as replacements. Back then they brought them in for injuries only. Nowadays it seems as if it's a twenty-three man game. I get a bit confused watching on television sometimes.'

Eoin laughed 'But don't get disheartened,' continued his grandfather. 'I'm sure your coach knows what's best for the team, which means he'll have you right in his sights. Keep working at your skills and you'll be in a good position when you are called upon.'

Eoin thanked his grandad for the advice and made his farewells. 'I have to go meet Dylan,' he explained. 'But I'll see you before we go back to Castlerock.'

Chapter 20

EOIN jogged down to Schillaci's, where Dylan was already tucking into a bag of chips.

'Here, Eoin, I've got loads and I won't finish them. I'll share them with you,' he offered.

'Thanks, Dyl. I don't think I could eat them either. I've done nothing but eat since I got home.'

'Same here,' answered Dylan. 'Mam thinks I've lost a load of weight. I wouldn't be surprised with what they serve up to us most days in school.'

'Ah, it's not that bad,' said Eoin.

'C'mere,' said Dylan, 'I laughed meself sick this morning over you.'

'Why?' wondered Eoin.

'Well, you know Caoimhe is mad into making scrapbooks? She has one for Disney characters, and one for pop stars? Well she's only gone and started one for – Eoin Madden!'

'Whaaaaat?' said, Eoin, blushing, 'that's a bit weird.'

'I know, I know,' laughed Dylan. 'She said she was starting it for my rugby career – well my one game in the Aviva anyway – but I got a look at it yesterday and she's been putting in all your scores and reports – and she's got nothing on the Under 14s!'

'That's very nice of her. I never bothered to do that myself,' Eoin said.

'Well, she wants you to call up and sign the cover for her. She's terrified you're going to get famous and never come back to Ormondstown. You're the only celebrity she knows.'

Eoin laughed and snatched the bag containing the remainder of the chips from Dylan's hands.

'You snooze, you lose,' he grinned, taking off down the street at a pace he knew Dylan's shorter legs couldn't match.

Eoin zigzagged around the passers-by before hiding behind the statue of a long-dead patriot while Dylan caught up. He spent the time guzzling the last of the chips.

'Eoin … you brat … don't do that … again,' puffed Dylan when he finally arrived.

'If you hadn't eaten so many chips you'd have caught me,' laughed Eoin. 'Now, where's this celebrity autograph hunter?'

Dylan turned the key to open the door of his house and announced his presence with a 'Hi, Mam, I'm home'.

Caoimhe came downstairs first, clutching a large book.

'Hiya, Eoin,' she mumbled, 'would you mind signing my scrapbook?'

'Of course I wouldn't!' said Eoin, 'Can I have a look at it?'

'Eh, well … OK,' Caoimhe replied.

Eoin flicked through the pages. There were a lot of newspaper cuttings on the dramatic end to the Begley Cup final last year, and the even more dramatic happenings outside the playing arena on Lansdowne Road. There were also short reports on this season's Junior Cup games, and an embarrassing team photo that Eoin didn't even remembered posing for.

'Yeeuch,' he said, 'I look really gimpy out there on the end of the line. Lucky it was printed so small. And look, they got my name wrong. "Owen Maddren". Who's that?'

Dylan laughed. 'Come on there, big head. They'll get your name right as soon as you do something to make them notice.'

Eoin grinned and thanked Caoimhe for keeping the cuttings.

'Can I get a copy of some of those off you?' he asked. 'I'll wait till the end of the season when we've won the cup.'

Dylan threw a sock at Eoin and the pair collapsed into another playful brawl on the couch.

Mrs Coonan came in with a plate of still-warm scones and the trio tucked in. 'Thanks Mrs C,' said Eoin, 'We don't get scones as good as this in Castlerock.'

'Well I'll be sending Dylan up with a plastic lunchbox full of them for ye. They'll last a few days before they get stale. I'm worried about him – are they feeding you up there at all?'

'Yes, they are,' explained Eoin, 'It's just because Dylan does so much running around at training that he's so thin.'

Mrs Coonan laughed. 'Well Eoin, I hope you're keep-ing an eye on Dylan and are making sure he does his school work!'

Dylan grinned lamely, 'Don't worry about that, Mam. You keep sending up the scones and I'll keep getting the As'

Eoin looked at his watch and stood up. 'Thanks Mrs C, that was lovely, but I have to be getting back. See you tomorrow, Dyl. We'll get the half two bus, OK?'

Chapter 21

. . . .

WHEN they got back to Castlerock there were just three more days before the Junior Cup semi-final, and Eoin was getting very nervous. Nobody wanted to talk about anything else around the school, even the teachers. It had been more than ten years since Castlerock had even been in the final, so none of the pupils had ever experienced that thrill.

'I wish it was over,' he told Alan as they walked between classes. 'I don't even know if I'm on the bench. Mr Carey is being very quiet about that. We have a run-out today and hopefully he'll let us know afterwards. I suppose if I'm not in the squad then at least I'll get a good night's sleep. At the moment I'm not even getting that.'

Alan paused. 'Look, it would be great if you get in the team, but it's no insult not to be picked. These guys are a year or more older than you. Even the small amount that you've done will be so useful for our year next season.'

'That's funny,' said Eoin. 'Dixie told me something

similar. Are you guys comparing notes?'

Alan laughed. 'C'mon we have History next, hope you have some progress to report on for the project.'

Eoin shrugged his shoulders and grinned.

In the classroom he was required to give a bit more detail however, and he told Mr Dunne that his researches had gone well and he had lots of information about the short life of Kevin Barry.

'That's fine, but you need to find out some more about what drove him to join the rebels and to give up his life in the way he did,' the teacher said.

Mr Dunne told the boys they had one week to finish their research work and they would have to have the project completed after the Easter holidays.

Alan groaned, and whispered to Eoin that he 'hadn't done a tap' on his project yet.

'How's yours coming along?' he asked after class. 'Any chance you could give me a hand?'

Eoin shrugged and laughed.

'OK, Alan, I'm training every day, studying the rest of the time and sleeping when I get a chance. I have a huge match coming up, maybe two. And I have my own project to do! If you have any ideas for when I can find the time to help you then I'd love to hear them. Because if you do then I intend to use that time to sleep some more.'

Alan smiled. 'Ah yes, I suppose when you put it like that …'

The training session was brief, just a run around and a few key moves repeated to make sure everyone knew their role. St Benedict's were a powerful force in schools rugby and the outside world was starting to pay attention to the game, with regular articles appearing in the newspapers.

'Right, men,' announced Mr Carey as the players completed their warm-down. 'Gather around.'

More than thirty boys each took one step forward. At this stage in the season the starting fifteen pretty much picked itself, but there were four or five other players in the same boat as Eoin, waiting to see if they'd make the match-day squad. Eoin was so nervous that his tummy felt very wobbly indeed.

'We have the most talented bunch of Js in all the time I've been here, but this week's game will be the first real test you will face. Benedict's are a tough bunch, very physical, and they will try to win the battle in the first ten minutes when they will go in hard for every tackle. We need to be cleverer than them, and try to withstand the pressure and tire them out. And then we need to play to our strengths, which means fast ball from the half-backs and letting our back-line run when the time is right.

'I've talked to Devin about our selection, and we've made plans for a livelier bench than the St Ultan's game. We've got Eoin back and I'm bringing back Darren McGrath as well to cover the wingers. They'll come in for Paudie and Keelan. Any questions?'

Eoin lowered his head, desperate to ensure he didn't catch Paudie's eye. Devin came forward and said a few words too, but none of the boys felt any need to ask questions. They knew what they had to do.

Chapter 22

· · · · · · · · · ·

EOIN knew he needed to be distracted from all the well-wishers and the junior school kids who just wanted to come up and stare at any member of the JCT. He pulled his grey hoody over his head, and slipped a notebook and biro into his pocket before exiting the dorm as quietly as possible. As soon as he left the building he broke into a canter, crossing the playing fields to his secret glade.

The light was already starting to fade, but Kevin was where he usually was to be found, scrabbling around at the base of the Rock.

'Hello, Kevin,' Eoin began. 'Have you found what you're looking for yet?'

Kevin stood up and shook the grass and earth from his ghostly clothes. His old rugby shirt looked like it had spent an hour under a ruck.

'No, I haven't,' he sighed, 'and I still don't even know what I'm looking for either.'

'Can I help?' asked Eoin. 'I have about an hour and we can chat while we're digging. I need to ask you about what made you join the rebels.'

'Righto,' replied Kevin, glad to share the burden of the digging. 'You take that area to the left and I'll keep going over here. Now, let me see …'

Once Kevin got started he talked freely about his days at school and how he had come around to the rebels' way of thinking.

'Where my mother came from in Carlow they were always talking of the 1798 rebellion that happened in the area. I used to go down there every summer and the songs and stories of the old battles would always come out whenever there was a get-together in the house. There was no television or radio then, which I believe keeps you youngsters busy for many hours a day. So we sat around and heard these heroic tales of men and women who took up arms for Ireland.

'Then the 1916 Rising came and it was brought right home – almost to our door in Fleet Street. The school I was attending, St Mary's, closed down that year and I was sent up to Belvedere College. Every day I walked past the GPO and drew inspiration from those men.

'One of the seven leaders of the Rising, Joseph Plunkett, was a past pupil of the school and his was a name you heard quite a lot around the place. They started playing hurling there and I joined up – my pal Eugene

Davy played the game with me. He was a great rugby player too – your friend Brian Hanrahan told me he played with him at Lansdowne and watched him play for Ireland. That would have filled me with pride.

'We played on the JCT together, but I didn't get to play in the final in 1917. They left me on the bench, sadly. I had scored a brilliant try – if I say so myself – in the semi-final at Lansdowne Road so they gave us all a winners' medal.

'I was getting very interested in politics around then, and later that year I joined the Irish Volunteers. I didn't get up to much, just cycling around delivering messages between the different battalions. I kept up the sport, though – it was great camaraderie and kept me fit, and I played senior my last year in Belvedere.'

Eoin continued digging away at the earth, pausing to make notes as Kevin went on with his life story.

'I did well at the books, and won a scholarship to University College to study medicine. But I wasn't much of a student to be honest. I enjoyed the dancing and the social life around the college a little bit too much – one day I fell off my bike four times cycling home after having a bit too much fun. I played a bit of rugby too, and joined up with the Old Belvedere club when that was founded for the former students.

'I kept up my activities with the rebels, of course, and our company was very successful at raiding factories and depots to get weapons and ammunition. I was made section commander and one day I was given a special job to do. We needed more weapons if we were to have a chance of taking on the Empire, and we learned that there would be a band of soldiers guarding a bread lorry taking supplies to the barracks.

'It was a routine operation, we thought – I planned to be back in UCD to do an exam a few hours later – but something went wrong and a shot was fired. That led to more firing but my gun jammed twice. I dived for cover under the bread lorry but my comrades all escaped and I was dragged out and captured.'

Eoin scribbled away as Kevin paused his excavations.

'Well, they had a trial of sorts for me, but sure I knew I was done for from the minute they captured me. Three of their soldiers lay dead and I knew they'd be wanting revenge for that. I felt sorry for them … They were all around my age. But I believed they should never have been in my country and so I had no option but to see them as my enemy.'

Kevin wiped his brow and stared off into the distance.

'They said they'd let me off if I gave up my comrades, but a man who gives up his fellows isn't much of a man in my way of thinking. So six weeks later they took me out of my cell one Monday morning, and then, well ... you know the rest,' he sighed.

Eoin stopped digging and flicked a bead of sweat from his face. 'Thanks, Kevin, I know that must have been hard to bring that up from so long ago.'

They silently returned to their work, but after a short time Eoin looked at his watch.

'I just have five minutes more Kevin. Then I'll have to call it a night. It's nearly dark anyway, I can hardly see what I'm ...'

Eoin stopped digging. His fingernails had hit something hard and he shook his hand to relieve the pain. He bent closer, and started to brush the clay away from where he had hit. He reached in again, and caught hold of a piece of metal. He pulled, and it came up with his hand.

Chapter 23

. . . .

'**W**HAT have you got there, lad?' asked Kevin.

'It's a big key, I think,' replied Eoin. 'It's covered in muck.'

Eoin rubbed at the key to clean it, showing it to his ghostly companion.

'That's it,' said Kevin. 'That's what I was looking for. It's come to me now. I wonder what it's for?'

'I bet I know,' came a third voice from behind the bushes.

Brian stepped through the greenery, his eyes bright with excitement. 'I'll warrant it's for the door in the secret room in the school!'

'Do you know, I think you could be right,' said Kevin. 'I kept getting flashes telling me where to look and how to dig. And there was a big, dusty door in the visions too. But ...'

'But what?' asked Eoin.

'But ... I don't think this is going to open that door. I think there's something else going on. I just got a flash of the front door of my old school too …'

'Why don't you hurry back to the dormitory, Eoin,' said Brian. 'You and Alan can check out whether the key fits or not, and Kevin and I will work out what to do next. I'll call by before school tomorrow.'

Eoin took the key and scarpered back to the main buildings as quickly as he could. It was quite dark now and that part of the grounds wasn't lit. 'Sure what are you afraid of,' he laughed to himself. 'You've just spent the last hour with two ghosts!'

He nipped into the bathroom on the first floor to wash his filthy hands and to remove the rest of the clay from the key. It was dulled by the years it must have spent underground, but a few seconds scrubbing brought a shine to the handle and Eoin reckoned it was a very important key back in its day. It might even still be.

Slipping the key back inside his hoody, Eoin strolled out to the corridor where he bumped into Richie Duffy and two of his hangers-on, Sugrue and Flanagan.

'You're looking a bit scruffy, even for a bog-man,' Duffy sneered. 'Were you out digging potatoes on the farm?'

Eoin grimaced, not wanting to rise to the bait. He grunted and went to squeeze pass Flanagan.

'Hold up a second there, Madden,' started Duffy as his

sidekicks blocked Eoin in. 'I hear you've been snitching to the teachers. You'd want to be very sure of your facts before you go making wild accusations.'

Eoin shrugged again.

'And how are things in the happy dorm? All hunky dory now that the thief has been caught. Or did Coonan get away with it and fool you all? Think about that, Madden. He's obviously planning to go into the family business when he finishes school.'

Eoin moved again to squeeze past Flanagan and this time he got through. He had wanted so much to say something, and was even ready to get involved in a scrap if that was what was needed. But he knew he had to keep the key safe and out of the hands of Duffy – who had been down into the secret passage and would surely work out what it was for, just as Brian had.

Back in the sanctuary of the dorm, Eoin found that only Alan had opted for an early night.

'Dyl and Rory have made it up and they're playing table tennis the last two hours,' said Alan.

'OK, quick, hop out of bed and give me a hand with the trapdoor,' asked Eoin. 'I think I've found the key to open that door on the left.'

Alan got out of bed and twisted the rose on the fireplace to open the passageway.

Eoin moved the trapdoor away and stared down into the dark hole.

'Here's a torch, Eoin, do you want to lead the way?' asked Alan, nervously.

Eoin made his way carefully down the staircase. It was harder to see as the torchlight batteries were running out and, in truth, his mind was racing as to what might be behind the door.

The boys stopped at the wooden door, and pointed the torch beam at the keyhole. Eoin slipped the key inside and turned it, but the lock didn't budge.

'It's too loose,' he told Alan, 'This key isn't meant for this lock.'

'I'm gutted!' Alan replied, 'I was sure we we'd discover amazing treasures.'

'We might yet,' Eoin grinned. 'And I think I know where to look next.'

Chapter 24

· · · · · · · · · ·

NEXT morning Eoin called down to the Rock to pass on the bad news, but neither of his ghostly friends were anywhere to be seen. He tore a page from his notebook and scribbled a quick note, telling them where he was going to try next. He tucked it in under the boulder where he hoped Kevin would find it.

School dragged slowly, but at least Mr Dunne was happy with his progress on the history project. It was half-day Wednesday, but with the cup final around the corner Mr Carey was keen to ensure there were no more injuries so they went through a light session before working on their fitness and stamina.

As soon as rugby was over and he was showered and dressed, Eoin nipped out the school gates and headed for the Dart station.

He bought his ticket and sat in a window seat to get a good view of Dublin Bay as they raced into the city centre. As the train went behind a row of hedges, Eoin closed his eyes.

'Where are you off to then?' came a whisper.

Eoin opened his eyes to see Kevin and Brian sitting opposite him. Eoin turned his head to check that no-one was near him in the almost-empty carriage.

'Did you follow me?' he asked.

'Yes,' said Kevin. 'Brian here spotted you dashing off and he came to get me. Luckily enough we can run a lot faster because we're dead.'

Kevin looked around. 'This is a very strange railway carriage. It moves a lot quicker than the old Kingstown Express too.'

Eoin grinned. 'I'm off to your old school to see if I can find out more about this key.'

Kevin frowned. 'Do you know, I haven't been back there for many, many years. But I suppose I can show you the way.'

Eoin got out at Connolly Station and followed the map he had called up on his phone. As he expected, Kevin was completely lost as the city's landscape had changed so much. They turned right onto a street that climbed steeply to the top of a hill.

'Ah, I recognise this now,' said Kevin. 'This has hardly changed a bit.'

They rambled up the street, gazing at the beautiful old doorways and colourful window boxes. Kevin looked up as they neared the top of the street.

'That's my old school,' he sighed. 'Happiest days of my life, or so they told me. What are you planning to do, Eoin?'

'I thought I'd try to find the Belvo equivalent of Mr Finn,' he said. 'He might be able to help. Are you two going to tag along? Try to keep it quiet.'

Eoin rang the bell on the big, black doorway, and waited while someone came to open it.

'Hello, I wonder can you help me,' he started. 'I was looking for the school historian ...'

'Well, young man, I'm the school archivist, so perhaps I can help?' said an elderly man dressed in black.

'It's a complicated story,' Eoin began.

'Well, you'd better come in and tell me then,' he smiled. 'I'm Brendan. What's your name, and is that a Castlerock jumper I spy under your jacket?'

'It is,' said Eoin. 'I'm Eoin Madden, I'm a student out there. I was doing some, eh, research and I found this old key. I've been led to believe that it has something to do with Belvedere.'

'And how were you led to believe this?' asked Brendan.

'Well, I can't really say yet,' said Eoin. 'I was wondering if you had any idea what connection it has to your school?'

'Hmmm,' said Brendan, 'I'd have to think about that.

114

There is one mystery in the archive that I've never quite understood, though. Come with me.'

He led Eoin along a corridor, where his Castlerock gear drew some hostile glowers from other boys. Brian and Kevin followed, and Eoin grinned as he imagined what the Belvo boys would do if his ghostly pals suddenly appeared to them.

Brendan showed him into a large room lined with bookcases and filing cabinets. He walked to a glass case in the middle, and Eoin was startled to see a series of artefacts to do with Kevin Barry, including an old browning photo of him charging up the wing at what was labelled 'Lansdowne Road', but looked nothing like the Aviva Stadium.

'This cabinet concerns the school in the years from 1916 to 1922,' Brendan explained. 'I'm sure you've heard of Kevin Barry, who was a pupil here, and these other items also come from around that time.'

He reached inside and picked out a wooden chest about the size of an egg box; Eoin spotted that Kevin had suddenly taken interest in what they were looking at.

'Here it is,' Brendan smiled. 'This was hidden in the archives for many years. It was found with a note saying it had been delivered in the dead of night during the

War of Independence and that it came from another Dublin school. It's locked tight and no-one ever got to the bottom of it. I wonder is this anything to do with your key?'

Eoin gasped. Kevin and Brian had just reappeared behind Brendan and were closely examining the rest of the contents of the display case.

Eoin took the key from his pocket and poked it into the keyhole. He turned it, and was delighted when it clicked and the little chest sprang open.

'Oh my goodness,' said the elderly archivist. 'That was a great surprise. Let's see what's inside.'

He lifted the lid, and there, lying on a purple velvet cushion, was another brass key.

Chapter 25

• • • • • • • • • •

'I THINK I know what that's for,' Eoin said, carefully. 'There's a lock back in Castlerock that's been unopened for years. Could I possibly borrow it?'

'Well … I'm sure there's no harm in that, since you're the one who found the key to open it after all these years, but I'll have to get in touch with your headmaster to tell him. It's Mr McCaffrey still, isn't it?'

'Yes,' replied Eoin. 'Or maybe Mr Finn – he's the archivist – would be better?'

'Well, maybe, if you think he might know what the key unlocks …'

Brendan disappeared for a few minutes to call Mr Finn, and came back with a smile on his face.

'Mr Finn told me you were the boy who won the Young Historian Competition, and you probably had a very good reason to borrow the key, so here it is. You will look after the key, won't you? We would like it back when you're finished.'

Eoin slipped the second key into his pocket and thanked Brendan before exiting through the front door.

Again he was startled to see Kevin and Brian standing outside.

'Well, what do you think?' he asked after the door closed behind him. 'I'll bet you any money the key fits the secret doorway.'

'Well, I think you're probably right,' said Brian. Kevin nodded, too.

'Did you see the exhibition they had about me in there?' he asked. 'It actually felt a bit embarrassing. There was a report saying I was too serious – what rot! They even had one of my school copy books with my scribbles all over it.'

Eoin laughed. 'I suppose I'd better be careful that all my schooldays stuff is safely locked in the attic before I ever get famous!'

The three wandered down the street. Eoin said hello to a funny-looking gentleman who doffed his straw boater hat and waved as they passed.

The ghosts disappeared after Eoin got onto the train, which was now packed with people travelling home after work. He felt the key poking into his leg and wondered what lay behind the mysterious doorway.

As he walked up the drive to Castlerock, Mr Finn opened a window and called out, 'Mr Madden, can you come up to see me, please?'

Eoin waved in reply, and jogged up the steps.

Mr Finn had a small office on the first floor where he was researching the history of the school. The desk was a jumble of stacks of books and papers that resembled the Manhattan skyline, and in between them Eoin could just about see the elderly teacher.

'Eoin, what is this all about?' he asked, 'The Belvedere archivist phoned to tell me of your visit.'

'I found a key in the grounds here, sir, and well, I was led to believe that it had something to do with that school,' he began. 'And sure enough when I went into town to Belvo we discovered that it opened a chest. Inside the chest was another key, which I think could fit the lock in the door in the secret chamber under our dorm.'

'I'm still not sure what you're talking about at all, Eoin,' Mr Finn said. 'But I do love an adventure and I suppose there's no harm in trying the door.'

The two walked up the stairs to the dormitory, where they found Alan lying on his bed reading a zombie comic. 'Hello, Mr Finn,' he said, jumping to his feet.

Eoin waved a key at him and grinned. 'I think I have it,' he told his pal.

The boys combined to open the trapdoor, and Eoin switched on the torch which lit up the room below with a yellow, flickering light.

'The torch is running low, Mr Finn,' he explained. 'We'd better hurry.'

Eoin led the way down, followed by Mr Finn and Alan. He went straight to the door and found the lock.

'Here goes,' he said, gently pointing the key into the lock and twisting. The lock groaned, and Eoin gave it another twist.

'It may be rusted,' said Mr Finn. 'Here, let me try?'

But just then Eoin grunted an extra effort and the lock responded with a loud '*clunk*'.

The torch faded just a little more as Eoin looked back at the teacher.

'Will I open it, sir?'

'Go on, you've come this far. Be careful though, there may be little furry creatures running around in there!'

Eoin pushed at the door, which was stiff and required some extra shoulder, but once it moved it swung open with a creak.

It took him a couple of seconds to get used to the dark, and he realised the torchlight was almost spent. There was some light coming from the wall to the right, where an ancient window frame was allowing some of the evening sunlight through. He stepped carefully over to it, unsure of what was underfoot.

'My, oh my,' said Mr Finn, following him into the chamber. 'This is a bit like what those archaeologists who discovered Tutankhamun's tomb must have felt.'

Eoin noticed that there was a small hole in the corner of one of the panes, but carefully used his sleeve to rub away at the window, removing decades of dust and grime. The sunlight flooded into the room.

Mr Finn stood open-mouthed in the middle of the room which was packed with boxes of papers, as well as some large wooden crates which were nailed shut.

'I think we need to call the gardaí, sir,' said Alan.

'Oh, I'm sure there's no need, this is just a lot of forgotten old rubbish,' Mr Finn replied. 'There may be plenty of interest for my researches of course, but I can't imagine what else there would be.'

'No, sir, look over by the window,' Alan insisted.

There, leaning up against the wall, stood a rifle.

Chapter 26

· · · · · · · · · ·

EOIN and Alan froze, staring at the weapon. They had seen rifles before in museums, but never in real life.

'Gosh, you're right, Mr Handy,' said Mr Finn. 'Eoin, come away from that wall, and don't touch that gun.'

The light outside had started to fade, but Eoin took one last look out the window. There was a good view of the small glade of trees where the Rock stood. He thought he saw a flash of red and yellow but it disappeared just as soon as he noticed it.

Mr Finn ushered the boys out of the chamber, and pulled the door behind him.

'Alright, you two,' he motioned to the boys as they climbed back into the dormitory. 'I'm going downstairs to get the headmaster, and some batteries for that torch. Please don't go back down that hole again.'

Eoin and Alan sat on the edge of their beds, their minds racing at all that they had seen.

'What do you think is in those boxes?' asked Alan.

'I don't know, but they look very old,' replied Eoin.

'I wouldn't say anyone has been behind that door for a hundred years.'

Eoin peered down the steps. 'I wonder why Kevin was so drawn to this school. He seems to know more than he's telling us.'

Mr McCaffrey walked in, with a very grave expression on his face.

'What on earth has been going on here, Madden?'

He stared down into the secret chamber. 'Has this anything to do with the mobile phones you said were stolen?'

'Well, sir, that's how we first found this room ...' Eoin started.

'Show me what you found, Mr Finn. You boys remain up here,' the headmaster snapped.

Eoin and Alan waited while the teachers went down to the hidden chambers. They returned within five minutes.

'Madden, Handy, I'm afraid we will have to move you to other quarters tonight,' said Mr McCaffrey. 'I will have to call the gardaí and they will be very disruptive coming through your room. Gather up your baggage and everything you need for school tomorrow and we'll find beds for you and the other pair. Handy, will you go and locate your room-mates?'

After Alan left, Mr McCaffrey sat down and looked Eoin in the eye.

'Neither Mr Finn nor I are quite sure what is going on here, Mr Madden,' he started. 'But I intend to get to the bottom of it. And what is this about you going in to Belvedere College?'

Without mentioning the ghosts, Eoin tried to explain how he found the first key and why he went to the other school to retrieve the second, but even he realised he sounded ridiculous.

'You just had "a feeling" that there was a key that fitted the lock down there?' asked the headmaster. 'And you expect me to believe you?'

'Well …' he stammered.

'Eoin is a very honourable, truthful boy,' interjected Mr Finn. 'I'm sure he meant no harm here and he may have done us a great service if those boxes contain what I believe they do.'

'Well, at least one of the crates seems to be full of rifles and ammunition,' started the head, before stopping himself from revealing any more. 'Pack your bags Mr Madden and I'll meet the four of you at my office in fifteen minutes,' he ordered. 'And please stay nearby this evening as I'm sure the guards will want to talk to you.'

Eoin did as he was told, and Mr Finn helped him

to pack. 'Don't worry, Eoin,' he said. 'Mr McCaffrey is naturally concerned for the school. But it will all blow over soon, I'm sure. I must confess that I'm quite excited as I think the papers down there are from the missing years of the school archive.'

Eoin smiled and lifted his bag off the bed. 'Thanks, Mr Finn, glad I could help. I know my story sounds a bit mad but I hope it all works out well in the end.'

Alan, Rory and Dylan arrived just as Eoin was leaving and he filled them in briefly on what was happening. 'We have to be at the headmaster's office in ten minutes, so hurry,' he said. 'Mr Finn will explain while you're packing.'

Chapter 27

· · · · · · · · · ·

MR McCaffrey found some empty beds in one dorm for Rory and Dylan, but Eoin and Alan had to make do with the spare room in the headmaster's own house on the grounds. His wife cooked them an enormous supper, but Eoin's appetite wasn't equal to the task of finishing it.

Mr McCaffrey arrived just as the boys were halfway up the stairs to bed.

'We'll talk tomorrow,' he said. 'The gardaí aren't too concerned with what they found at first glance. It all seems like ancient history. But Mr Finn is certainly excited by it all.'

Eoin slept poorly, his mind turning over what had happened and how he had tried to explain it. There were still many answers he needed hidden in that room.

Next morning he found it hard to concentrate on his studies. Mr Dunne had to call his name twice to get his attention.

'Mr Madden, are you with us?' he asked, sarcastically. 'Or dreaming of scoring a match-winning try in the semi-final again?'

Eoin returned a thin smile and went back to his book. He had actually forgotten about the game, which was now just twenty-four hours away. He needed a good run after training tonight.

The last run-out of the Js team was shorter than usual. Mr Carey took each of the units through their moves and even subbed Eoin and a couple of others in for some play towards the end. Maybe he intended to give him a few more minutes in the semi-final. The team were relaxed, with plenty of laughing and joking, even when Devin said a few words. Mr Carey was the victim of some mickey-taking too as Zach Cooper hid his tactics board in the showers.

As the team rambled back to the school afterwards, Eoin slipped away and set off at a trot towards the woods. He pushed his way through the low branches and sat down on the Rock to catch his breath.

'You look exhausted,' said Kevin, coming out from behind the Rock.

'Well, I hardly slept last night and today I've had a full day at school AND rugby training. I'm flaked out,' Eoin snorted.

'How did the key work out?' Kevin asked.

'Well, it opened the door, but I was hardly in there for

two minutes when we had to get out. There was a load of rifles hidden in there. Imagine, we were sleeping over an arms dump all year!'

'Rifles, you say?' asked Kevin. 'Were they in wooden crates?'

'Yeah ...' replied Eoin, 'Although there was one loose rifle, standing up against the window.'

'Anything else ...'

'No. Just some boxes of papers, I think. It was very dark though and it was all a jumble,' said Eoin.

'Let me know what they find, won't you?' insisted Kevin.

Eoin nodded and went to ask the ghost a question, but before he opened his mouth Kevin had disappeared.

Eoin jogged twice around the rugby pitch before he headed over to his temporary home. He didn't want to meet Mr McCaffrey and was happy when his wife opened the door and told him that the headmaster was out at a meeting.

'He's out with that lovely Mr Duffy. He is so generous to the school, you know. Do you know his charming son, Richard?' she asked.

Eoin winced, and nodded, but didn't want to get into a conversation about his least-favourite schoolmate.

Alan was sitting at the kitchen table in front of the

last slice of an apple tart. 'Ah, Eoin, I kept you a piece,' he grinned.

Alan patted his stomach and smiled again. 'Fantastic meal again tonight, Mrs Mac. Do you think they might need us to stay here till the end of the school year?'

Mrs McCaffrey smiled. 'I'd be delighted to have you. It's great to have a bit of company around again since our boys went off to college. And every slice of apple tart you eat is one less for me. I'll make another one now so you can have it for breakfast.'

'No thanks, Mrs McCaffrey,' said Eoin. 'I'll just have something light, maybe a sandwich. I've a big game tomorrow and might need to move a bit quicker than Alan.'

Chapter 28

. . . .

THE semi-final was a grim battle, decided by an excellent individual try by Zach Cooper, but despite the result the Castlerock boys went back to school with glum faces; as they climbed onto the coach to take them back to school, an ambulance pulled out and took off up the road with its siren blaring. On board was Ronan, who had taken a heavy hit late in the game and looked like he had badly damaged his ankle.

Eoin came on to replace him at out-half and did nothing wrong in the eight minutes before time ran out.

'Well played, Eoin,' said Devin as he passed him on the bus. 'That was a tricky situation but you kept your head. See you at training tomorrow – we've a lot of work to do now before the final.'

Eoin smiled, and turned his head to the window as the captain moved away. He was still tired – he just wasn't used to a mattress as soft as that on the McCaffreys' spare bed – and dozed off.

In his dream he was running up O'Connell Street in Dublin city centre, and was weaving through piles of rubble. As he passed the General Post Office he heard a bullet whistle past his ear, and called out 'Don't shoot, I'm just going to school'.

He woke up suddenly, to the sound of laughter. Paudie and Gav were leaning over the backs of the seats in front of him.

'What's that about "don't shoot", Madden?' Gav laughed. Are you dreaming about a gangster film or something?'

Eoin went bright red and turned away from the pair. He must have been asleep for quite a while as the bus had just pulled into the grounds of Castlerock. As they neared the door there was a disturbance up the front as several boys stood up.

'What are they doing there?' asked Devin.

Eoin stood too, and was a bit taken aback to see two garda cars, an ambulance and a large white truck parked outside the dormitory building.

The bus stopped and the players filed off and collected their kitbags from the storage area underneath. Mr McCaffrey, who had been talking to a senior garda, walked over to congratulate Mr Carey.

'Well done, boys, I understand it was a notable win,' the headmaster addressed the team. 'I'm sorry I wasn't able to attend the game but I will be sure to be at the final. I'm afraid I was tied up with an important matter here at the school.'

Mr McCaffrey stopped and looked from face to face through the players. 'Ah, there you are, Mr Madden. Would you mind coming with me?'

Eoin's face turned red for the second time in five minutes, and he had no choice but to follow the head-master across the driveway to where a man in a dark-blue uniform stood.

'This is Eoin Madden, guard,' said Mr McCaffrey. 'He is the boy who discovered the mysterious chamber.'

'Ah, the adventurer!' said the garda. 'My name is Inspector Corbett. I wonder could you tell me the whole story up in the room.'

Eoin followed the garda upstairs, and was surprised to see the dormitory had been barred off with plastic tape on which were printed the words 'CRIME SCENE'.

'Am I in trouble, sir?' Eoin asked.

'No, not at all. I understand you have only been in the room for a minute or two?'

'Yes,' replied Eoin quickly. 'Mr Finn was with me all the time.'

A man dressed in an all-over white suit with a hood and mask came up the steps into the dorm, followed by another. They carried two long wooden poles between them which looked just like a stretcher, covered with a rough green blanket.

A third man climbed into the room as they left, and acknowledged the senior garda.

'Ah, Inspector,' he said. 'We've quite an interesting one here. A complete skeleton, still wearing some type of uniform. It has rotted away and there don't seem to be any sort of identifying papers.'

'A body!' gulped Eoin, 'underneath our bedroom?'

Chapter 29

. . . .

'**D**ON'T worry, son, he's long past worrying about,' smiled the inspector.

Mr Finn arrived at the door.

'Good afternoon, guard,' he said. 'I'm a retired teacher at the school and a friend of Mr Madden's family. If you want to talk to him I'd like to be present.'

The inspector nodded. 'Of course, that would be appropriate. But Mr Madden has nothing to fear. This poor man has been dead almost a hundred years.'

'I was with Eoin when the room was opened for the first time, and we left very promptly,' Mr Finn pointed out.

'Ah yes,' replied the garda. 'Well perhaps you could tell me did any of you touch a rifle that was standing near the window?'

'No,' said Mr Finn. 'As soon as we saw it we left immediately, realising that the guards would have to be called.'

'Good,' said Inspector Corbett. 'It's just that, on first examination, there appears to be a whiff of cordite from the barrel.'

Eoin looked puzzled.

'I'm sorry, I should explain,' said the Garda. 'What I meant to say was that, from the smell off the rifle, it appears to have been fired very recently indeed.'

Eoin gulped.

The garda noticed the change in Eoin's expression.

'Do you know anything about that, young sir?'

'Well, no, I don't know anything about who fired the rifle,' Eoin started. 'But a few weeks ago I was out for a run when I heard a couple of shots. I thought they were coming from the school but I wasn't sure.'

'And did you report this to anyone?'

'No,' said Eoin, sheepishly. 'I wasn't certain and I thought it was probably a car back-firing or something.'

'And where were you precisely when this happened?'

'I was out near the woods, over there,' he pointed out the window.

The Garda asked Eoin and Mr Finn more questions about the opening of the room, and seemed to be happy with the answers.

'Can I ask you a question?' asked Mr Finn.

'Fire away,' grinned Inspector Corbett. 'I'm not sure I can answer it but …'

'What exactly is in those boxes?'

'Well, it's mostly papers. We'll have to check, but

135

there doesn't seem to be anything in them except some old school records,' he explained. 'I suspect they were being stored here for safe-keeping. There is also a case full of brand-new rifles — well, they would have been brand new a century ago anyway — and plenty of ammunition. There's also another big wooden chest which I didn't want to break open but our locksmith is working on down there now.'

'And who is the dead man?' asked Eoin.

'We haven't a clue. You heard the doctor — he has no identification papers on him, and it will take ages to check our files for missing persons when we don't even know the decade in which he died.'

Eoin frowned. 'I've been studying that period in school,' he said. 'I think if you look around 1920 you could be lucky.'

The inspector stared at Eoin. 'That's very interesting,' he said. 'You're obviously a very clever young man. We'll give it a go.'

'Inspector!' came a call from below. 'I've lifted some fingerprints off the rifle. And guess what, they're fresh!'

Inspector Corbett grimaced. 'Are you gentlemen sure you didn't touch that gun?'

Mr Finn stared back. 'I am, and I am just as sure that Eoin didn't touch it either. There must be some other explanation.'

'Well, would you be willing to be fingerprinted – just to remove you from our enquiries?' asked the garda.

'Of course,' said Mr Finn, and watched as one of the men in the white overalls produced a fingerprint kit. He and Eoin gave their samples and, just as they were about to leave, another call came from the basement.

'Inspector, we've got the trunk open,' said the garda who poked his head out through the trapdoor. 'It's an interesting haul.'

'Would you like to see this, Mr Finn?' invited the inspector, who then led the way down the staircase.

The technicians had lifted the chest out of the side room and opened it just at the bottom of the stairs, so Eoin could see down inside it. Even in the gloom he could see that it was packed full of silver cups and trophies.

Chapter 30

· · · · · · · · · ·

THE word spread like wildfire about the opening of the hidden chamber and the treasures that had been found there. Eoin's central role in the drama made him the focus of everyone's attention and he could barely walk two metres anywhere in the school without someone pointing to him or asking him a question. Even the teachers wanted to know about the discovery.

Eoin buried himself in his history project, which was just about complete, and in his rugby, which was a great way to escape.

There was less than a week to the Junior Cup final in the Aviva Stadium. Mr Carey was keen to forge a firmer understanding between Eoin and the scrum half Paddy Buckley, so there were even a couple of pre-school sessions with just the two of them and the coach.

'The Belvo wing-forwards are very fast on their feet,' explained the coach to Paddy. 'So you need to be even faster getting the ball out to Eoin.'

The two boys worked on signals, and the best pace and direction for Eoin to receive the ball.

As the three rambled back towards school, the school nurse, Miss O'Dea, was parking her car. She waved and called out to Mr Carey. 'I just want to warn you, Mr Carey, that I have had a serious outbreak of the vomiting bug among the third-year boys. There are three down at the moment, but I would like you to keep an eye out for symptoms among your players. Many of them will have some protection from illness but any that haven't could be in trouble.'

Mr Carey went white. 'Thank you, Miss O'Dea. That's very worrying indeed. Boys, back to school now, I'll see you at training in the afternoon.'

There was a full attendance at the training session, where Mr Carey asked all the boys how they were feeling. He also pressed on them that it was important to tell Miss O'Dea if they felt at all poorly.

Eoin returned to the dorm to meet Dylan and collect his bags for a brief visit to Ormondstown. The boys were old hands at travelling on the bus now and relaxed as it sped through the midland towns on the way to their home.

'Did you hear about the bug thing?' Eoin asked his pal. 'Carey's terrified that it will hit the team. I think he was glad to hear I was getting out of town for the weekend!'

'Do you think ye might need a winger?' asked Dylan. 'Especially one with try-scoring experience at the Aviva. You know what they say about horses for courses?'

Eoin laughed. 'It's going to be hard enough without having you out there on the wing. Anything planned for the weekend?'

'Caoimhe wants to go to the movies tomorrow night. Would you be up for that?'

'Ah, sure why not. I haven't seen a movie in ages,' Eoin replied.

The boys parted at the bus-stop, where Eoin's dad was waiting in the car. Dylan lived just a short walk away. 'See you tomorrow Eoin. Call for me about six?'

On the way home Eoin filled in his dad on as much of the drama about the secret room as he could without spilling the beans on the ghosts.

'My, oh my, that sounds very exciting. And the gun had been fired? I hope you weren't in any danger?'

'No, Dad,' laughed Eoin. 'I think it's all a bit of ancient history.'

Eoin's mother was even more concerned, but he soothed her worries and explained that the gardaí had taken everything away for examination.

He weekend in Ormondstown began quietly. Eating, sleeping and visiting his grandfather took up the bulk of his time, but he also helped his dad to paint the shed and washed the car too. After dinner he jumped up from the table to collect the dishes and rolled up his sleeves to start the washing-up.

'What's all this eagerness to do the chores?' quizzed his mother.

'No reason,' smiled Eoin. 'Always happy to help.'

'Are you looking for a few euro for your cinema date tonight?' laughed his dad.

Eoin blushed. 'That's very kind of you to offer Dad,' he grinned. 'A tenner? Perfect.'

His dad laughed. 'A tenner's about right for all the work you did. Leave those dishes and get yourself ready. I'll drop you down to Dylan's.'

Chapter 31

· · · · · · · · · ·

THE movie was a bit of a disaster. Not a disaster movie, but a terrible film about stupid people doing unbelievable things. They laughed at all the serious bits and Eoin and Dylan took turns to make fake-vomiting noises when the actors were attempting to be funny. Caoimhe and her pal, Daniella, were very amused by their antics.

'You could be a comedian, Eoin,' Caoimhe laughed at one stage.

They were still laughing as they left the cinema, and wandered down the town together in great spirits.

'Are you coming up for the game next week, Caoi?' asked Eoin.

'I don't think so. Mam only goes to watch Dyl's games,' she replied.

'Sure he might be playing yet. There's a terrible dose of the winter bug in the school and they could need him.'

Caoimhe chuckled. 'On the Junior Cup team? Little Dyl? That'd be hilarious to see. I suppose he could run through their legs ...'

And with that she took off, laughing as went, avoiding her brother's clutches.

They ran about fifty metres before both stopped, panting, outside the chip shop.

'C'mon lads, anyone for a sausage and chips?' asked Dylan.

'Not for me,' said Eoin. 'I've been eating all weekend and the chips aren't a good idea if you want to keep an athlete's physique like mine.'

Dylan grinned and nodded. 'Do you know what, I think you're right. Now, race you to the supermarket, we'll have an apple instead.'

The following afternoon Eoin walked down to see Dixie in his home. The old man had a cold and was sitting wrapped in a blanket when he called.

'I've had this dose for a couple of days, but I'll make sure I'm right for my annual trip to Lansdowne Road for the final,' he smiled. 'I hear from Andy that you've been impressing some people in the Leinster set-up.'

'Really? I hadn't heard that ...' replied Eoin, puzzled.

'Oh, perhaps I've spoken out of turn. Or maybe I was mistaken,' said Dixie.

'Sure I've only played for a few minutes here and there this season,' Eoin replied. 'That game in Rostipp was the only time I got a full game.'

'Well, I suppose it doesn't take long to show your class,' he chuckled. 'But have you the stamina to last a full game next week?'

Eoin smiled. 'To be honest I'm not sure. I've trained hard but it has been frustrating to get so little time in the middle. I hope I'm up to it.'

Dixie wagged his finger. 'Eoin Madden, you're a fantastic player, and I should know. You must ensure you have confidence in yourself because it will come out in the way you play. Playing at outside-half means being able to make quick decisions and acting on them instantly. If you lack self-belief you won't play as well as you could. So don't ever forget your previous great games and how you were able to set up scores for Castlerock.'

Eoin smiled. 'Thanks, Grandad, I'm sure I'll be fine. This will be my third time to play in the Aviva and it's still a bit overwhelming. And all the guys I'm playing against are a year or more older than me.'

'But none of them have your experience in Lansdowne Road,' Dixie pointed out. 'You have two winners' medals from two games there – I know some top-class rugby men who went through whole careers without winning even a match there, let alone a medal.'

Eoin thanked his grandad and gave him a hug. 'I'll see you next week then, hope you get a good seat.'

'Oh I'm sure Andy Finn has a nice comfortable one for me in the royal box,' Dixie laughed. 'I'll give you a wave.'

On the bus back to Dublin Dylan was hyper with excitement. Caoimhe had mentioned Eoin's suggestion that he might get on to the team due to the bug outbreak and he was already planning his tactical approach to playing in the game.

'Steady on, Dyl!' pleaded Eoin. 'I was only saying that to Caoi to encourage her to come to see the final. There would need to be a lot of guys out for you to get in the team.'

As soon as he said it, Eoin realised that he probably should not have. Dylan glared at his friend and, obviously hurt, turned his face to the window and put his earphones in.

Chapter 32

· · · · · · · · · ·

EOIN was right, of course, but even he couldn't have expected that so many of the squad were laid low by the bug. Mr Carey called over to the dorm on Sunday night to check that his out-half was still in his full health.

'Thank goodness,' he sighed. 'Six of the starters and three more of the squad are in the sick bay. I've asked the Leinster Branch for a postponement but they won't grant it. Something to do with it being on television and tickets being sold. Thankfully they've allowed us to register some extra players from outside the 35 so we can at least turn out a team.'

Mr Carey turned to survey the rest of the room. 'Ah, Dylan Coonan,' he said. 'We are a bit short of wingers. Can you turn up at training tomorrow?'

Dylan nodded. 'Do you need Rory too?' he asked.

'Well Gav O'Donnell is out, so you might as well bring him along as cover,' the coach replied. 'And if you see Charlie Johnston could you ask him too?'

As soon as Mr Carey had left the room Dylan leapt up

on his bed and did a somersault as if it was a trampoline.

'Yahoo!' he cried. 'That's awesome news. And Rory too!'

Eoin smiled. 'And of course Caoimhe and your mum will have to come up too.'

'Yes, I forgot that,' replied Dylan. 'But maybe I should wait to see how training goes?'

The news of how Castlerock's squad had been seriously depleted hadn't reached the ears of the media just yet, which was why it wasn't mentioned in the preview of the game in *The Irish Times*. During first class on Monday Mr McCaffrey called in to the science lab to read the article aloud to the boys:

I would venture to say that the clash of Castlerock and Belvedere in this week's Junior Cup Final could be a classic collision of styles. In the cauldron of Aviva Stadium this could, assuredly, be a titanic battle in the trenches. Belvedere's golden generation are, as ever, enigmatic, but Castlerock are the sleeping giant of les temps perdu and thus worthy of respect.

Interestingly, the latter entity has had its hand forced by fate and have had to pluck a second year into its ranks for the big day. The versatile Eoin Madden has put his hand up for selection, been hauled off bench duty and gets the nod for Le Grand Match. He is sure to step up against his school's traditional bête noire.

Eoin felt his face turning bright red as several of his classmates turned to stare at him.

'Well, Mr Madden, it appears you are considered "versatile",' said the headmaster. 'Well, good luck on Wednesday and I'm sure the boys wish you well in your "titanic battle in the trenches",' he chuckled.

There was plenty more ribbing throughout the day, and it didn't stop when Eoin turned up for training after school. Because so many of the players had cried off, Mr Carey had to abandon his plan for a light work out in favour of a full session to introduce the replacements to the team's tactics.

The team were so short of wingers that Dylan was given a chance to try out against a boy from the 15Cs. Dylan was far quicker than the older player and after his second try Mr Carey told him to join the first team group.

Eoin felt sorry for Mr Carey who was looking very hassled by the late disruption to his plans. Another one of the front rows had pulled out that morning and the coach was now most concerned that the school would

not be embarrassed by a hiding at the hands of Belvedere.

Devin had avoided catching the infection but even he
was starting to despair. He played number eight but both
the wing-forwards he packed down alongside were now
sick in bed and he was struggling to explain the calls to
Charlie and the other forwards who had been drafted in.

After training was over Mr Carey asked them to return
the next day for another attempt to work on some plans.

Eoin walked back to the school with his room-mates.

'It's so much faster,' gasped Rory.

'And they're so much bigger,' gulped Dylan.

'And that's why I'm in this team since the start of the
year – and you only got in when there was an outbreak
of plague,' joked Eoin as he broke into a jog.

But as he rounded the corner he was brought up
quickly by the sight of the headmaster in deep conversation with Inspector Corbett.

Chapter 33

• • • • • • • • • •

'**A**H, Mr Madden,' called out Mr McCaffrey. 'The Inspector here has some interesting news about our unfortunate mystery resident. Let us go into my office.'

Eoin followed the teacher and the policeman, and stood at the door as they took their seats.

'I'm afraid the mystery has actually got a little deeper,' explained the garda. 'We were able to take some very clean fingerprints off the rifle that had been recently fired, and our technicians came up with a match in our records. The strange thing was, however, that they were for a man who had previously come to our attention – or more accurately, the attention of the police force of the time – way back in 1920.

'His name was Eugene McCann and he was one of those who were arrested for attacks on British Army premises during the War of Independence. He was part of a well-known gang who seized weapons and we think those cases of arms are from one of those raids. We have experts from the National Museum working on the case with us,' he added.

Mr Finn arrived at the door of the headmaster's office and stood beside Eoin as the policeman continued his story.

'It seems McCann disappeared sometime in 1920 and nobody ever found out why. There was one theory that he had been murdered by soldiers, another that he was shot as an informer, a third that he had fled to Canada. One way or another, his body was never found – until you and Mr Finn came across it,' he added.

'It will be good that the man will get a proper burial,' said Mr McCaffrey. 'But has anyone any theory why he might have been holed up in Castlerock?'

'I think I might be able to help there,' replied Mr Finn. 'I have been writing a history of the school,' he told the Inspector, 'and I have been a bit hampered by the fact that a large portion of the school records are missing, particularly from around ninety to a hundred years ago. But I had discovered that one of the senior teachers was quite sympathetic to the rebellion and had even taken part in some of the activities. I suspect this gentleman may have been willing to allow the arms raiders to hide their haul in the school. He presumably used the "second key" ruse for security. Perhaps the records will be able to tell me more.'

'Well, that's very interesting,' said Inspector Corbett. 'And I've brought you back those boxes of documents. We were unable to find anything relevant but then you would be much more familiar with the characters and the times. Please let us know if you find anything.'

Mr Finn smiled and thanked the policeman, and just as he and Eoin were about to leave, he asked one question that had occurred to him.

'That gang that Mr McCann was a member of – were there any other members' names in your files?' he enquired.

'Oh, yes,' replied the Inspector, 'And one quite famous one too – a lad of eighteen summers called Kevin Barry.'

After dinner, Eoin went up to his room and lay on his bed staring at the ceiling. His mind was full of the Junior Cup final, his history project, and the meeting with Inspector Corbett. His usual solution to such a situation was to go out for a jog, but he was tired after training – and it was lashing down anyway.

He realised there were so many questions he wanted to ask Kevin, but they would have to wait for now.

'You look like a man with the weight of the Castlerock Rock on his shoulders,' quipped Alan, as he rambled into the dorm. 'Nervous about the game?'

'Not particularly, to be honest,' Eoin replied. 'No, I'm

up in a heap over the secret chamber and all that. The body the guards discovered turns out to have been a comrade of Kevin's. I've been convinced Kevin never told me the full story all along.'

'Why don't we go down there again?' asked Alan. 'Maybe this other guy will be there too?'

Eoin shrugged, and swung his legs off the bed.

They worked the contraption that opened the trap-door and made their way down the steps, Eoin leading, carrying a fully-charged torch.

The heavy lock lay on the floor outside the secret room with the key still inside it. Eoin pocketed it, remembering his promise to the Belvedere archivist. Inside the room he shone the torch into the four corners, hoping to see something that would help, but the chamber had been completely cleared by the gardaí.

'Looking for someone?' spoke a familiar voice, and Eoin pointed his torch in the direction from which it came. The light caught the famous black, red and yellow jersey of the Lansdowne club.

'Brian! You gave us such a fright!' gulped Alan.

'I'm a ghost, that's what we're supposed to do!' laughed Brian.

Eoin grinned too, but that was wiped from his face as two other shimmering figures stepped into the room.

He recognised one as Kevin, but the other man was a stranger.

'Howya, Eoin,' said Kevin, sheepishly. 'I believe I owe you a bit of an explanation. But first I'd better introduce you to an old comrade of mine. His name is Eugene.'

Chapter 34

• • • • • • • • • •

'AND I think I owe you an apology lad', said the third of the ghosts, a curly-headed man about the same age as Kevin, but quite a bit shorter. 'You were the fellow I had to shoot at a while back, weren't you?'

Eoin nodded.

'Well, as Kevin will explain, I had to warn you away from that part of the grounds,' said Eugene. 'I'm really very sorry about that, but I'm a pretty good shot and I always aimed about ten yards above and wide of you. You were never in any real danger.'

Kevin cleared his throat and looked at the boys. 'I'm very grateful for your help, lads, and Eugene is too. You've helped him more than you will ever know. As you learned in school, and in that project of yours, Eoin,' Kevin went on, 'I was a member of the rebels back in the day. We were in no position to take on the Empire at the time, but I and a few of my comrades were given the job of building up our store of guns and ammunition. We did right well on a few of those raids, but we had terrible problems storing them and keeping them hidden. The police and army were always raiding our homes and those of anyone connected to us.

'Then the brother of one of the senior men in the rebels got a job as headmaster here in Castlerock. He was sympathetic to our aims, but had never been involved. He was one of the few who knew about this secret room and he allowed us to store our weapons here.

'One day we raided the King's Inns and got a huge haul of rifles. We were getting nervous that they might be discovered or stolen so we put a man here to guard them. That was Eugene. We locked the door from the outside so no-one could stumble upon the weapons.'

His comrade took up the story. 'I stayed on guard for a few days, and then someone else took over. That went on for a month or two. One day, a man in Kevin's platoon locked that big door behind him and left me here with enough food and drink for three or four days' duty.

Kevin spoke again, looking mournful, 'I was asked to go on another raid and that was the one that did for me. When I was in Mountjoy awaiting my fate one of my comrades, an old school pal, Joe Memery, came to visit disguised as a priest. He told me that he'd left Eugene on guard, locked into a room in Castlerock over a week before, but thought he was being watched and so had been unable to get out to the school to check on him. We were always terrified of spies and informers – not to mention being stopped on the street and arrested – so rather than keep it in his pocket he had put the Castlerock storeroom key in a small wooden box and locked it.

'Joe hid the key to the box under the Rock out there and cycled into town to our old school. One of the brothers that taught us in Belvedere was very fond of him and when he asked him to look after the box he did so, no questions asked.'

Eoin smiled, remembering his detective work and the visit to Belvedere.

Kevin continued, 'Well, Joe said he was going to try to get out to Castlerock and he headed off and, well, a few days later my time was up. My sister came to visit, and a couple of priests from school. On my last night, not long before dawn and after I had said goodbye to my family, the priest was praying and he said a prayer for Joe Memery. I stopped him and asked what he meant and he told me that Joe had been found shot dead in an alley not far from the jail a few days before. I knew then that he had been discovered after coming to visit me.

'I also realised what this meant for Eugene. I feared it was already too late for him, but I was still desperate to get a message to someone about the keys but there was a warder there and I wasn't able to make the priest understand ...'

'So what happened to Eugene?' asked Alan.

'Well, like the brave patriot that he was, he stayed at his post. He never knew Joe had been murdered, so he stayed here until the end.'

Eugene nodded gravely. 'I don't remember much about it at all. I was desperate for Joe to return and I just kept hoping that someone would come to rescue me. Once or twice I considered breaking the window and shouting for help but I had orders and I wasn't going to break them and give myself and the weapons up. The hunger and thirst was terrible and after a while I got very ill. I suppose I just didn't wake up one morning. The next thing I heard was some youngsters scrambling about at the door. I went out and gave them a bit of a fright with a few wooooo-ooooos,' he laughed. 'They dropped everything and ran.'

Kevin spoke again. 'It was Eugene's spirit stirring that brought me back to Castlerock. I was frantic trying to find that key out there, but it's hard to move the earth quickly when your fingers aren't made of skin and bone anymore,' he grinned. 'Happily you were able to help me out.'

'I was on duty at the window a while back when I spotted Kevin,' explained Eugene, 'and I knew then he was back to find that key and then to relieve me. When I saw you out there too I was afraid you would find the key instead and I'd never be at rest – so that's why I fired those shots. They passed way over your head, but I wanted to frighten you off. I don't think they worked!'

'Yeah, it was a bit scary for a second,' admitted Eoin. 'The police are very confused that the gun was fired even though the door had been locked for ninety-something years!'

'Still, it'll give you something to write about in your project won't it?' smiled Brian.

'I don't think so,' replied Eoin. 'If I mention ghosts nobody will believe a word I've written. But Kevin has been great too, and he's given me loads of information.'

'Glad to be of help, lad, and now we had better go.' Kevin replied. 'Eugene deserves a break from this place after such a long time. I do hope we get to meet the pair of you again someday,' he added before the three ghosts began to disappear.

As he left, Kevin gently tossed a small brass object towards Eoin. 'Here, is this any use to you?'

It was the bullet casing that he had picked up on Sackville Street during the Easter Rising in 1916.

'Wow, that's *amazing*,' said Alan, when Eoin told him where it had come from. 'Another gift from the ghostly world to top off another prize-winning project.'

Chapter 35

· · · · · · · · · ·

MR CAREY was in a terrible state. His bout of pre-match nerves was usually worse than any of the players', but the vomiting bug outbreak had made him even more edgy. On the bus to the ground he walked up the centre aisle examining the eyes and faces of each of the players for signs of illness.

'Mr Carey!' called out the headmaster 'You really need to relax. I'm sure the boys will let you know if they aren't feeling well. It looks to me that the worst thing they are suffering from is nerves, and I'm not entirely sure you are helping to cure that.'

Eoin laughed. He was very relaxed himself. Having Rory and Dylan along was a great help, and Charlie Johnston was also there representing the year below on the Castlerock team. The fact that they had lost so many players was disappointing, but it also removed a great weight of pressure from the remainder. They weren't expected to win now, and knowing that allowed them to approach the game with less stress.

The bus pulled into the stadium and parked alongside

that of the Belvedere team bus, which had just arrived too. Eoin scanned the faces of the adults who accompanied the team but the archivist, Brendan, wasn't among them.

Castlerock had been allocated the home team dressing rooms and Eoin took that as a good omen – they had used them on his two previous finals there. They changed quickly and went for a run out on the field, watching the stands as the supporters trickled in wearing scarves, hats and jerseys of black and white or green and white.

Eoin spent most of his time trying place kicks from different angles, trying to gauge the wind direction in a stadium where it often swirled around in circles. Dylan helped him collect the balls in the netting sack and the pair waved at their families as they walked off the pitch.

As they reached the dressing room they sensed a new mood, and it wasn't a good one. Mr Carey was rushing about and Rory was standing beside the door with his face almost pure white with shock.

'What's going on?' asked Dylan.

'It's Paddy,' said Rory. 'When we came back in he started throwing up. He's in the bathroom there.'

'Oh no, that means–'

'Yeah, I'm playing,' gulped Rory.

The teams ran out onto the pitch with the stadium announcer telling the spectators 'In a late change to the line-up in your programme, Rory Grehan will replace Paddy Buckley on the Castlerock College team.'

Eoin hung back to the end of the line, and patted Rory on the head as they left the tunnel. 'You'll be fine, Rory, stay cool and enjoy the day. No need to be nervous – you've played here more than any of the Belvo lads.'

Rory grinned. 'Hey, good point. I never realised that. Good luck yourself.'

Dylan was right when he had remarked a couple of days before that his new team-mates were so much bigger than the Under 14s. And the Belvedere boys seemed bigger still.

Eoin's previous playing visits to the Aviva Stadium had been when Castlerock were the support act for a big Leinster game, so the ground wasn't as full now as it had been then. But there was still a huge crowd keen to see the old rivals battle it out.

Devin won the toss so Eoin got to start the game – he always preferred to kick-off. He took his time, propping the ball up and awaiting the referee's instruction.

'Let's go,' said the man in the yellow shirt, before releasing a loud blast on his whistle.

Eoin kicked the ball high, hoping it would hang in the air and give the Castlerock forwards time to get underneath. It worked out perfectly, with the Belvedere catcher instantly submerged by a wave of green and white shirts. The crowd roared their approval – it was always important to win the first play. Better still, the tacklers took the ball off the Belvo player and quickly funnelled it back to Rory.

The scrum-half was quick to get the ball to Eoin, whose kick into the far corner skimmed across the pitch like a flat stone and bounced into touch. The Castlerock supporters roared once more, sensing there could be points to be had from this amazing start.

At the line-out Devin soared in the air and caught the ball with both hands, as his team-mates gathered around, they drove towards the line. The Belvedere forwards were clearly shocked at how they were being pushed back by a smaller, lighter pack before they even had time to settle into the game.

Castlerock were just a couple of metres from the line. Rory stood with his hand on Devin's back, and glanced back to Eoin who was staring him in the eye. Eoin nodded and flicked his eyes towards the ground to the right of the pack.

Rory got the message. As the maul inched forwards

Eoin took off to his right, distracting the Belvo cover, which moved to follow him. Rory grabbed the ball and dived for where the gap had opened up on the line. Twisting his body like a salmon he thrust the ball forwards and it hit the ground just over the white-washed line.

'*Prrrreeeeeeeepp*,' went the referee's whistle, and his right arm shot straight up into the air.

Rory, who was buried beneath a pile of black-and-white-shirted bodies, took a while to emerge but was soon swamped by another cluster of green and white shirts.

He grinned at Eoin and mouthed 'thanks' before handing him the ball. Eoin propped it up on a tee and steadied himself for the kick. From the stands he heard a cry of 'Go on, Eoin!' from a familiar voice. He looked over to where Caoimhe and his own family were seated and grinned. Back he stepped and thumped the ball right between the goalposts.

Chapter 36

. . . .

A SEVEN-point lead with less than two minutes gone is a pretty good start in any game. But Eoin was afraid that Castlerock may have just galvanised their opponents. Belvo were a powerful side and they would regroup from this setback. Their power meant they could expect to win more possession, and Castlerock's main job would be to ensure they didn't convert that into points.

Belvedere hit back hard, and Castlerock didn't get out of their own half for the next twenty minutes. But a dropped pass allowed Eoin to gather and he found touch just beyond half-way. Zach had taken a knock so the rest of the players took the opportunity to drink some water and grab a few seconds' rest.

'We just need to keep making the tackles,' said Devin, who had himself been covering more ground than anyone on either side. 'Don't let them get a glimpse of our line. We can do this.'

Devin again won the line-out, and this time Eoin went for a garryowen. He kicked the ball high into the

166

air and as their full-back caught it, Eoin followed up fast and floored him with a tackle. The Belvedere man didn't release the ball however, and the referee awarded Castlerock a penalty which was well within Eoin's range.

The half-time whistle blew soon after, and as they jogged off Devin pointed at the scoreboard. 'Pinch me, someone,' he said, 'I would have laughed at you if you had told me we'd be ten-nil up at half-time.'

Despite the scoreline, the Castlerock dressing room was a grim place at the break. The tackles had taken a toll, with several players nursing aches and bruises and others trying to rest their battered bodies. Mr Carey and Devin spoke about keeping up the same level of commitment and making sure they didn't make any silly errors in their own half.

Eoin slipped into the bathroom for a moment's peace but he didn't get it.

'Hello, Eoin, you're playing well,' came a familiar voice. Eoin turned to see Kevin and he noticed that he was still wearing his black and white Belvedere jersey.

'I thought I'd show my colours today,' he smiled. 'I hope you don't mind. Although I would prefer the College to win, I've become very fond of Castlerock in recent months.'

Brian, too, appeared and congratulated Eoin on his

fine display.

'You're probably standing too close to the scrum-half,' he suggested. 'That lad has a good pass and if you stand back a couple of steps you'll have more options to go on the attack.'

Eoin nodded. Brian had always come up with some great advice during games. He'd have a word with Rory.

'Thanks, lads. I'd better go now,' he grinned. 'I hope you're cheering for Castlerock, Brian?'

'Of course,' grinned the ghost. 'Never liked those Belvo boys from my own schooldays.'

Eoin smiled to himself and left the pair having a bit of banter about times long past.

Chapter 37

• • • • • • • • •

THE team were already filing out of the dressing room, so Eoin grabbed a quick drink and jogged out at the back of the line. It had started to rain during the interval and the wind had picked up too.

Rory looked at the sky as they prepared for the Belvedere out-half to kick off. 'Looks like it could get worse,' he said, pointing at the black clouds that were moving in their direction.

The Belvedere team looked as if they had been given a serious talking-to at half-time, and seemed determined to get back into the game from the first kick. Their forwards swarmed after the ball, and pounced upon it quickly. With Castlerock on the back foot, the Belvedere scrum-half chipped the ball over their heads and set off at a gallop after it. Eoin turned quickly but he was already two metres behind the little No.9. He chased hard, and made a powerful flying tackle, but the Belvedere player's momentum took him over the line for a try.

Devin was furious as the Castlerock team stood wait-

169

ing for the conversion. 'They caught us while half of you were still in the dressing room,' he fumed. 'We need total focus for the next twenty-nine minutes, and anyone who's not willing to do that should walk off right now and let me bring on someone who is.'

Devin's mood was improved slightly when the Belvedere kicker badly hooked the ball wide, but the team in black and white were energised by their score and came roaring back on the attack. They spent the next ten minutes camped inside the Castlerock 22 but Devin, Charlie and Aaron Douglas led the way in repelling their attacks.

A knock-on gave Castlerock a scrum, which gave Eoin the chance to kick the ball upfield and relieve the pressure. Devin gave him a thumbs-up as they trotted into the Belvo half for the first time since the interval. 'If we get a sniff of a chance to kick points, you should take it,' he told Eoin. 'An eight-point lead would make it just a bit more comfortable. We can't hold out forever.'

Eoin nodded and took Rory aside – he had a plan to get within range. As Brian had suggested, he stood a couple of metres further back from where he usually would be, and when Rory fired the ball back he was already moving at speed. The momentum carried him through the first couple of tackles and suddenly he was facing the Belvo full-back, a giant of a boy.

Eoin tried the sidestep that had been perfected on the field with Ormondstown Gaels, but the No.15 was ready for it and brought him down into the mud with a thumping tackle. Eoin rolled and released the ball, and Rory put his hand on it and grinned at him. 'Watch this, bud,' he said, before firing it back to Dylan who had taken Eoin's place at out-half.

Eoin watched with horror as the little winger took the ball and with one easy movement, dropped it to the ground and kicked. The ball sailed high in the air before dropping over the bar.

The referee's arm shot up, but the Castlerock players were too stunned to notice. After two seconds of silence Devin started to laugh. 'What were you doing, you little pup? That could have gone anywhere!'

Dylan grinned back. 'But it didn't, did it? Straight down the middle and three points for the Rock.'

Eoin laughed too. 'Have you ever dropped a goal before?'

'Eh, now that you mention it … no,' gulped Dylan. 'It was Rory's idea. I just didn't think about it.'

With the score at 13-5 the Belvedere boys needed to score twice and they knew it. A couple of heads had drooped with Dylan's drop goal and they seemed to lose heart as time ran down.

The stadium clock showed that less than two minutes were left when Belvedere won a penalty inside the 22, and their kicker converted. The sudden realisation that they now had a chance to snatch a win gave them a huge boost, and when the Castlerock kick-off went to ground they charged into the ruck.

The sheer ferocity of the attack rattled Eoin's team-mates and soon the ball emerged on the Belvo side. The black-and-white backs lined-up, ready to go on the attack, while Castlerock's steeled themselves to repel one final attack. Eoin took a quick glance at the giant scoreboard where the clock was ticking down: 12, 11, 10, 9 ...

The Belvo out-half made a break before passing the ball out to his centres, who were powerful runners and broke through their tackles. Suddenly it was three against two, and the Belvedere backs flicked it on to their winger. He had looked very sharp earlier in the game, but this was his first chance to run. He took off and was just a metre from touching down when a green and white blur came in from his left-hand side. It was as if a hand grenade had been lobbed at the winger as he was sent flying by the thumping tackle, and his body folded in surrender as he tumbled over the touchline in defeat.

The referee put the whistle to his lips for the last time and sounded an end to the thrilling contest. The Belvedere winger stood up and shook himself down before patting his tackler on the head.

'Well done,' he admitted. 'That was some hit.'

Dylan looked up, dazed, and grinned. 'Is it over? Did we win?' he asked.

The sight of fourteen players in green and white charging towards him gave him his answer.

Chapter 38

• • • • • • • • • •

THE sight of Devin lifting the famous old trophy was the sweetest thing Eoin had seen in a long time. 'No pressure, but that'll be you next year,' quipped Rory.

The team sat around the dressing room for half an hour, just enjoying their win and reliving the moment when Dylan dropped his goal. The little winger tried to drop-kick plastic water bottles into a waste basket but failed with every single one.

As Eoin was leaving the dressing room he was stopped by a tap on his shoulder. It was Brendan, the Belvedere archivist who was accompanied by Mr Finn. 'Congratulations, young man. That was a great performance today, although you will forgive me for not cheering you on. I heard from Andy here about your discoveries and I look forward to sharing some information with him.'

Eoin produced the key from his pocket. 'Thank you, and apologies for not delivering this back before now, but I just didn't have any spare time.'

Mr Finn smiled. 'Brendan was telling me that Belvedere was recently presented with a photograph of one of their former pupils scoring a try out on that field there, and he has given us a very nice copy for our own archive.' He opened a large brown envelope to reveal a photo of a boy in black and white sprinting over to score at Lansdowne Road in the days when there was a grand-stand on only one side of the ground. Eoin smiled and gazed down at the historical figure who had shared his love of rugby and become his friend.

'That's Kevin Barry,' said Eoin, 'I've been doing a project on him in history.'

'I have something for Brendan too,' said Mr Finn, producing a hardback notebook. 'This is the record book of the rugby teams at Castlerock, with all the results and teams from the earliest days. There are some marvellous names here, including the same Master Barry playing for Belvedere.

'Maybe you could borrow these items for your presentation,' said Mr Finn, 'you certainly deserve it.'

'I'd like that,' said Eoin.

Eoin joined his family for a few minutes and was delighted to see how happy Caoimhe and her mum were that Dylan had been the hero of the day. It was a relief to share the spotlight.

Dixie shook Eoin's hand and smiled. 'I've been talking

to a man here today who was asking me lots of questions about you and your rugby. In fact, he's standing right behind you …'

Eoin turned and was surprised to see a man in a blue and white rain jacket with a white harp on his chest.

'Well played today, son. I was very impressed. I've been watching a few of your games this season and I wonder would you like to get some coaching at a higher level,' he asked.

Eoin wasn't quite sure what the man meant, and must have looked puzzled because the newcomer laughed.

'I'm sorry, I should have introduced myself, of course. I'm the head of youth rugby with Leinster. We'd really like you to get involved with our academy.'

Eoin was stunned, and didn't know what to say. He looked past the man's shoulder where he could see two figures running around the field pretending they were still playing rugby many years after they had departed. Kevin and Brian stopped, and waved at Eoin.

'Say yes,' roared Brian.

'OK,' laughed Eoin, turning to the man. 'I mean … yes. Yes, please!'